TABBY TROUBLE

IRIS LEIGH

Contents

Thank you to my best friend Amy,
For if it wasn't for you I wouldn't have become a cat aunt to
three amazing but annoying cats who inspired this story.

Tabby Trouble Blurb

I don't ask for much, and I know for sure I didn't ask to communicate with cats.

But when I agree to cat sit my best friend's cats, that's exactly what I get for my trouble—well, that and a baffling murder mystery to solve.

Now my next-door neighbor is dead under mysterious circumstances, the talking cat is giving me orders, and my cat is missing, and somehow both are connected.

It's up to me to figure out how and why and solve the murder in a town full of potential suspects.

I'm going to need a little more than luck and a chatty cat to help me solve this puzzle, but there's one big problem. I've never solved a crime before, let alone investigated on

"**A**re you sure I was the only one you could ask?" I took in the mess before me, my once very clean living room no longer spotless as bags of cat food, a pail of kitty litter and a pile of carpeted wood pieces that somehow assembled into a cat tree lay scattered before me.

"Absolutely!" my best friend's voice chimed through the phone speaker. Her medium-length black hair was tucked back behind her ears and her dark eyes shone at me as we video chatted. I was sure she could see the unease in my body language as I tried to process everything, because her eyes definitely shined with the satisfaction of successfully tricking her best friend into watching her cats. Something I realized I should have probably said no to, the longer I looked at her. Her smile never wavered from her face.

One week ago, I was in the same exact position

talking to the same exact person. Except one week ago, I wasn't having to share my home with three cats. She couldn't have just one cat. No, she had turned into a crazy cat lady earlier than most and adopted three. When she wanted to travel abroad, she needed someone she trusted to watch her babies and somehow, I was the only one she could call. Or I was the only one gullible enough to agree to the request.

"I don't feel confident about this." I spoke softly as one the cats sat down right in front of me.

She stared at me like she wanted something. But since I didn't speak cat, I wasn't sure what that might be. Even though I'd been given the names of the cats, I had no idea which one was currently sitting in front of me.

"I can't tell who is who."

"It's easy! Turn the camera around, let me see which one you are looking at."

I maneuvered the phone so that that screen was no longer showing my face but instead showed the feline who sat before me. Her green eyes never left me as I tried to get her full form to display for my best friend.

"That's Luna! You can tell because she is the biggest of the three and has longer fur!"

Moving the phone away from the now identified cat that was supposedly Luna, I directed my friend's attention to a cat that could pass as Luna's twin, who was hiding in the corner. Upon arrival, the twin had scurried off and refused to remove from her spot.

"That is Zaira! She is smaller than Luna and her fur is about half an inch shorter, too."

My face scrunched in thought and I tilted my head while trying to process her statement. I took in the two cats, who weren't twins. How could she tell a half of an inch of fur difference between the two cats, especially over the phone?

"Fur that's half an inch shorter? Right...Whatever you say." Rolling my eyes briefly, I crouched to the floor to return Luna's stare. I pursed my lips and cleared my throat, doubts flooding through my mind as I wondered if I was going to do this correctly. Was it too late to back out and not be responsible for three additional bodies?

I wasn't much of a cat person. With dogs you waited for them to approach you, sniff you, and then the rest became history. Could the same be said for cats? Cats and dogs had to be similar. If not, this was a disaster waiting to happen.

"What are you doing?" my friend asked.

"Shh...I'm trying to bond."

Luna looked at me. She didn't take a step forward or attempt to smell me, she just stared. We stayed like that for a few moments—just one human and one cat analyzing each other. But in the end, she just walked away. No sniffing, no petting, no type of interaction. Absolutely nada.

Was it possible to be instantly disliked by a cat? Could she tell I was a dog person? Scratching my head briefly and pushing down the doubt that was steadily increasing, I turned to the next cat in sight—Zaira.

"You'll like me, right?"

Still crouched down to the floor, I wobbled a little closer toward her, but as soon as I moved forward, all that sat in front of me was empty space. One second she was there and the next second she wasn't. Blinking rapidly and looking around, I tried to replay the last few seconds, wanting to understand fully what had just happened. There was a gray cat with supposedly half an inch shorter fur with green eyes there one second, and then suddenly she was gone, like she could run at light speed.

"What the..." I muttered, looking at the now empty spot in front of me.

"Yeah, she's a fast one!" My friend's voice boomed through the phone as her laughter couldn't be contained.

I drew back and tensed up as I leapt to my feet as a loud bang followed by the sound of glass shattering rang throughout my home.

"And that's Lola. Got to be careful of that one, she can be a bit feisty."

I sprinted to the kitchen, where the loud noise had come from. Where I could only stand and gawk at the mess. The third cat, Lola, had jumped on the counter and knocked over my rack of clean dishes straight onto the floor. Utensils were strewn about on the floor and spanned from one side of the kitchen to the other. The utensils were intact but that couldn't be said for the millions of little shards of glass that gave my kitchen floor a twinkle. There wasn't a single piece of glassware that had survived the fall. Everything that was once on the counter was now on the floor.

Meanwhile Luna, absolutely oblivious to the mess she'd caused, sat perched on the windowsill above the kitchen sink, looking outside, totally content as her tail swished back and forth.

"You get used to it." My friend's voice rang out from the phone clutched within my hand, pulling me from the increased anxiety at the mess I would have to clean up.

Dragging my eyes from Luna and doing my best to skip over the huge mess that I would have to clean up but really didn't want to, I stared at the beaming eyes of my best friend through my cell phone. Her bright smile concealed the laughter that threatened to release but the slight twitch of her cheeks gave her away. She was amused at everything unfolding and at having tricked me into watching her crazy cats. Well, at least that made one of us amused because I was definitely not.

"I'll get used to it? You must be crazy!" I shook my head vigorously in disbelief and hollered out as Zaira poked her head into the kitchen to see what the commotion was all about.

But the cat who had caused the whole mess still sat perched on the windowsill, unfazed by the mess she'd made and especially unfazed by the shrieking human behind her. Which was me.

"I think I should go. Call me if you have any questions! I appreciate you!" And with those parting words I was no longer staring at my best friend but instead the home screen of my phone.

Did she just hang up on me? Pulling up her contact information I attempted to call her back, fully intent on sending the cats somewhere else, hopefully somewhere very far away, but to no avail. She didn't answer, At least one of us was smart.

Taking a look at Lola and then looking at Zaira, I spoke out loud to voice my confusion as if the cats could understand. "It's just us now, I guess."

Zaira bobbed away, and I was left staring at the empty spot on the floor that was once occupied by an animal with fur a half an inch shorter than her twin. I drew my breath in, held it, then released it as I tried to gather my thoughts. I repeated the steps a few times. Haunted by the days that would follow now that I was in charge of three cats.

"Why did I agree to this?"

Chapter Two

I let loose a yawn as my hand tried to muffle the next one begging to be let loose. The bags under my eyes were darker than usual, and my body felt sluggish. It was only the third day, but it felt like a million had passed.

If having cats was any indication of what parenthood would be like, then I was nowhere ready to be a parent. One eye open while sleeping was becoming a normal thing now, and it sucked.

Randomly through the night, I heard crashes and the ringing of the bells on their collars as they darted around the home.

Every morning consisted of cleaning up after the messes they'd made the night before and downing several shots of caffeine, which sent jolts of energy coursing through my body to try to overcome the lack of sleep.

And that is where I'd found myself on this Saturday —slouched on the couch ready for a nap despite it only being eleven o'clock. I was completely drained of all energy, and the day wasn't even halfway over. I groaned, hands coming up to cover my face as I let out a whine. The weekends were no longer appealing, now that I had several four-legged roommates.

Luna lay spread out across my lap, purring up a storm. It seemed like she never stopped purring. She liked attention, especially when it related to being brushed and receiving scratches.

But it was food that she loved most of all, as I found out very quickly. Any indication of a can opening and she was the first one by my side, weaving between my legs and purring, happy that it was feeding time. She would occasionally spend time reaching toward the countertop on her hind legs in her attempt to get closer to the food and to signal that I was taking too long to feed her.

She came running whenever it was or wasn't feeding time. She was easy and predictable to care for, probably my favorite of the bunch, but it had only been three days and things could change. Parents couldn't call favorites, but I wasn't a parent, I was just a cat aunt. And all aunts had favorites, even if they didn't outright say it.

Zaira and Lola were a different matter. I was still adjusting to them, especially Lola. Zaira was a zoomer and it was usually her bell that could be heard at odd hours of the day. Zooming from one end of the home to the other, finding and exploring every nook and cranny that she could fit her small frame into.

And then there was Lola. I shot a glance over in her direction. Again, she was perched at the window, her tail swishing back and forth as she peered outside from the dining room.

She was the boss of the house. She made it known every single day, and especially during the night. When she meowed at me, I already knew what she was saying. Sometimes it would be her displeasure at not being able to explore something. But the most common was the meow that meant she wanted the window open. So, the dining room window was left open often to keep her happy.

She was enchanted by the outside, and I would rather have a higher utility bill than a bunch of broken items needing constant replacement. So, the window stayed open.

It was only a matter of time before she figured out she could knock over electronics. I stared at the TV perched on its stand. Scenes of a crime about to unfold flashed before my eyes. The show was about to play out an unavoidable murder. Which reminded me I should probably mount the TV on the wall—better be safe than sorry, since Lola would eventually make her way to the TV stand.

The sounds from the TV barely registered, as I

wasn't really paying attention to the show. Just needed some type of background noise to help kill the buzz of my headache from having three cats as roommates.

Additional scenes flashed across the screen indicating the main character was finally going to get murdered. Now that grabbed my attention a little. I slid closer to the edge of the couch to peer closer at the screen as I waited for everything to unfold. My heart started to beat faster as the pace of the music increased, despite the volume being on low. The murder was inevitable now.

Any second now...any second now...

My body jumped and my heart almost burst from my chest as a loud *smack* followed by a few others in a quick succession, with an accompanying *hiss,* filled the room. Now that definitely had not come through the TV. My body was already tense from being ready to watch the murder play out on the TV show, but I hadn't been ready to be bombarded with noise in real life.

I took a few deep breaths to get my rapidly beating heart under control. Wrapping my hands around Luna in order to move her off my lap, I set her aside on an empty spot on the couch. She meowed her displeasure at losing her comfortable position, but I paid her no attention. The noise had to have come from one of the cats. I pushed off the couch, making my way over to the window. Zaira had also joined Lola and together they crouched down on the windowsill to look outside.

I peered outside to see what had caused the cats to freak out as I positioned myself to stand behind Lola and Zaira. First thing I saw was not one cat, but a group of them. There were three cats, to be exact. They stood on the edge of my yard, just watching us as we watched them. It was no longer morning but the afternoon now by the darkness creeping in, which gave the cats a weird glow.

I crouched down a little and pushed my face closer to the window. None of the cats looked familiar. It wasn't often that cats came to visit my home. They must have sensed that new cats had moved into the neighborhood and wanted to check them out. Odd, but cats were odd creatures, after all.

Since nothing exciting was going on outside, I turned around and settled back onto the couch and wrapped myself up in a blanket. Luna happily moved back into my lap once more to get comfortable, while Lola and Zaira continued to stare at the cats outside.

The murder scene had long passed in the TV show and now they were trying to figure out who among them had murdered the person. Sunlight was replaced by moonlight in my home by the time they figured out who'd murdered the guy. I looked over to the window to make sure everything was okay. I could see that Lola still sat perched on the windowsill, still completely enchanted by the outdoors. Meanwhile Zaira was nowhere in sight

Chapter Three

My head buzzed as loud sirens went off outside. Instead of the warm glow of sunlight filtering through my windows, it was replaced by a bright flickering red and blue light. Sundays were supposed to be days for sleeping in, but not this Sunday apparently.

I needed something to drown out the noise and light and the only things within reach were pillows. The pillow underneath my head was soon planted on my face in an attempt to regain some quiet, but it didn't work. Instead, the noise intensified as it seemed more vehicles arrived. What in the world was happening outside?

I did a few stretches to allow some energy to course through my body as I tossed myself out of bed. The bedside window had a view of the street so hopefully, I would be able to see what was going on outside. I peeked out, trying to identify what had caused this gathering of police and firetrucks.

All that greeted my quick peek outside was a row of emergency vehicles, blocking any attempts to see anything else. Frustrated at the lack of information and the interruption of my glorious day of sleep, I pushed my feet into some slippers and made my way through the house to go outside.

It wasn't cold out, but there was a nice breeze. It was fall, after all. I made sure I closed the front door behind me so the cats didn't escape. I stepped outside and scurried to where a group of people had gathered to see what was going on. Majority of the faces I recognized as people who lived on my block, which made sense.

It appeared something had happened to someone on the block though and that was bad. The only ones on the street that I couldn't match a name to a face were mostly those from the fire and police department.

In the throng of people, I could easily locate and make out the figure of my next-door neighbor. She was an elderly woman who was notorious for leading the gossip ring in the town. She knew everything and everyone in this community. Nothing escaped her watchful eyes and her need for gossip—skills no doubt developed from being married to a retired cop.

She spent so much time in his presence that some detective skills and instinct had probably rubbed off on her. She had a knack for gathering information about people—especially information they tried to keep hidden.

"Good morning Mrs. Higgins." I greeted the short lady with gray shoulder-length curly hair blowing softly in the wind. Her hazel eyes gazed my way, and I could already see the glint in her eyes. She was brimming with information and just waiting to share. It seemed like I would get my answers to what was going on sooner than expected.

"Oh, good morning, Kat! Did you have a wonderful sleep? How are your new cats?" Her voice rang out as people bustled about around us.

A police officer stood a few feet away talking to another neighbor while scribbling away in his pocket notebook.

"I did until all the sirens woke me up. The cats are adjusting okay, I think."

She nodded in reply before looking over toward the emergency workers who stood in the street with us. Some had already started the process of packing up their stuff to head out to the next emergency that was just waiting to be called in.

"Poor Rose, it wasn't her time to go."

To go?

Scratching my chin in thought, I attempted to remember any mention of her moving away. Gears turned in my head as I tried to figure out what Mrs. Higgins could have meant by "to go."

She must have meant that Rose had died.

Emergency vehicles wouldn't be called if she'd simply moved away. No, it must have meant she died.

I wasn't close to Rose Hastings like others who lived on our block, like Mrs. Higgins. It would be weird not having the ability to see her anymore and it would require some adjustment. But for her to die suddenly was interesting. I would need to gather additional information to piece together what had happened, so I focused my attention back on Mrs. Higgins. I was fully intent on figuring out what had happened to cause the sudden passing of Mrs. Hastings.

"Gone? Are you sure, Mrs. Higgins?"

"Of course I'm sure, deary! My information is never wrong!" She raised her hand to do a little finger wag to accompany her words at my doubt of her information.

If any government agency was looking for an undercover agent who had a few years on them, I could recommend the lady in front of me in a heartbeat. She was a master at gathering information for her gossiping ring, so no doubt she would know what had unfolded in the home across the street from our homes.

"Do they have any idea what caused her death?" I pressed further.

Rose Hastings hadn't looked like the type to kick the bucket anytime soon. She never complained about any health problems or even mentioned anything about being sick on the rare occasions we had talked. She was getting on in years but that didn't always equate to having health issues. With her random passing though, it reminded me that anyone had the potential to drop dead at any moment. Or so it seemed.

Mrs. Higgins leaned over, and since I was a head taller than her, she motioned for me to bend down to allow her better access to whisper in my ear. My knees bent more than a little to meet her height as she darted her eyes around trying to see if anyone was observing us. I also looked around, trying to see whatever she was looking for.

Everyone I saw was talking to someone else or complaining loudly about the emergency lights still flashing.

Why was she looking to see if someone was observing us? We didn't have anything to hide. Or, at least, *I* didn't have anything to hide. I was also pretty sure Mrs. Higgins didn't have anything to hide despite her weird behavior. She may be odd but she wasn't *that* odd that she would commit a crime on the same block she lived.

"They say it was a heart attack, but I don't believe them for a second!" Her words were hot against my ear as she tried to communicate quietly but with passion. Her eyes still darted about as she took in the scene again. Then they settled back on me.

"Surely if it wasn't a natural death the police will find the real cause of death?" I asked.

"Supposedly, but sometimes the best detectives are those who know you personally."

"But I don't know her that well."

"You've missed the whole point." With her final words, Mrs. Higgins turned on her heels and headed back home. I watched her as she crossed the street to the home that stood right next to mine. Every few steps she stopped and look around before continuing forward, as if trying to find something out of place. She sure was an odd one.

Now that my source of gossip was gone, I turned back to the emergency workers, who were pretty much all packed up and ready to leave. Everyone else in the street scattered as the emergency vehicles started to head out.

With the crowd thinning out there would be no point for me to stay outside as well. I headed back in the direction of my home.

I went to turn my front door knob when a rustling noise filtered through the air. My body tensed. What was that? The neighborhood was pretty safe, but with the death of Rose Hastings supposedly a murder— according to Mrs. Higgins, anything could be possible.

I slowly turned my head to the side to peer over my shoulder in a not-so-obvious attempt to figure out what the noise was from. But no one at eye level was behind me. I glanced about trying to see if I might have missed a person, but again I didn't see anyone lurking about. Satisfied that no one was behind me, I turned back to my front door once again to enter my home.

Before I could push the door open though, a soft

meow from behind me drew my attention. Was that the rustling I had heard? A little creature had padded out from within the bushes to stand behind me as I turned to face it. His orange coat stood out against the green backdrop of flowers and bushes.

"Hi, Rusty."

In order to be closer to cat level, I bent down and stuck my hand out to scratch behind his ears in greeting. Rusty was Mrs. Rose Hastings's cat, who must have gotten out with the chaos of the emergency workers coming in and out of the home. Now that his owner had passed away, he would need a new home. But I already had three cats, and I was not keen on adding a fourth.

"I can't let you in because I have three cats living here now. And I don't know how to introduce cats to other cats yet." My fingers continued to ruffle his fur while I spoke to him.

I stood up to head back inside, withdrawing my hand from petting him as I did so. Before bed I would set out some cat food and water for Rusty so at least he would be cared for tonight.

I would also need to talk to my neighbors to see if anyone could take care of him. Even though he was a half inside, half outside cat, I was sure he didn't want to be a full outside cat just yet. He acted a lot like Luna, who loved attention and food.

As soon I walked inside, I could see Lola eyeing the open door. I quickly closed the door as I looked at Lola.

I didn't want to leave it open too long, in case one decided to meet the other and a cat fight followed. Bending down, I scratched behind Lola's ears but she paid me no attention, her eyes still fully on the now closed door.

The death of Rose was still on my mind as I walked to the kitchen to make some food. As soon as the fridge door opened, Luna made her way over. I'd never had someone this close to me die before. It was an odd feeling. I wasn't sure how to act. We weren't close but she was a friendly neighbor that I would miss.

Luna let loose a soft meow that brought me out of my thoughts. It would be best not to dwell on stuff that couldn't be changed. I put the jam and orange juice on the counter and then grabbed the bagels from above the fridge and popped one in the toaster. A simple breakfast to start the day would be best and then I could figure out what to do with myself the rest of my day. Trying to stay productive and busy, I washed a few dishes while the bagel toasted.

Luna let out another meow, which broke my attention once more from the task at hand. As I turned to face her the toaster popped and I rushed over to grab my bagel before Luna thought it was a great idea to take a bite of it. But I knew instantly I had made a mistake the second one hand went to grab the bagel and the other went to unplug the toaster as a jolt of pain shot through my body.

My vision flashed in and out rapidly accompanied

by a falling feeling—or was I actually falling? Luna's face staring at me was the last thing I saw before my vision faded to black.

My mind started to go quiet as I faded out, but I wondered if I was going to be joining Mrs. Hastings.

Chapter Four

My chest felt heavy, like someone had put a brick on it and left it there. Which would make no sense, considering the fact I didn't have any loose bricks in my house. My head buzzed as the events of the day flooded back in.

Mrs. Hastings had died. Wait. I had almost died too! My body shot right up from its position on the floor as everything started to come back to me. I had almost died!

The sudden movement of sitting up caused another wave of pain to shoot through my body as I collapsed back to the floor. I looked over and saw Luna's eyes peering at me as she approached me lying on the floor. She must have been the brick I had felt moments ago. I should really put her on a diet.

Seeing that I was awake and no longer at death's door seemed to make Luna lose interest in me and she walked away. I stared at the ceiling of the kitchen and all I could think about was how I was such an idiot for touching a plug with wet hands. Drawing my fingers through my hair, I let out a heavy sigh. I would most likely have to buy another toaster and the outlet might be fried.

A soft steady knocking against the front door brought me back to focus. No longer reeling from the high of being electrocuted, I pushed my body up. It didn't hurt as bad as it had just a few minutes ago.

The sun was no longer shining into the house so it was safe to assume I had been on the floor for several hours. I looked through the little peep hole and didn't see anyone, but the soft knocks kept occurring.

Did getting electrocuted make ghosts real? Because if so, that would be cool! I'd always wanted to talk to one. Cracking the door open to see who could be knocking, I saw the face of Rusty.

Since it was someone familiar, I opened the door even more and crouched down to give Rusty some more ear scratches.

"Hey handsome, did you come to get some food?"

"No."

My head tilted to the side as I stared at Rusty. His mouth had definitely moved, but cats couldn't talk. At least not in words we could understand the last time I checked. There had to be someone else nearby who had talked to me, but looking about, I could not see anyone standing around.

"I must still be feeling the effects of being electrocuted," I muttered.

"Another dead human so soon? Great."

"Who is out there?" I called out as I shot to my feet.

My eyes darted about trying to locate the person who had yet again answered. But just like before, there was no one to be seen.

A flickering light at Mrs. Hastings house caught my attention. The little garden lights she put under her sign that stated she had the best lawn of the month flickered off and on, as if the bulbs were going bad. Other than that the night was still—no other movement except from Rusty, who was just a cat.

"Getting electrocuted causes you to lose your hearing?" the voice called out again.

I was one hundred percent sure there was not another soul nearby, so who could be talking? But it couldn't be Rusty, right? Setting my gaze upon him and dropping down to be as close to eye level as possible, I gave him a hard look. My eyes narrowed a bit as I spoke once more.

"Hello."

"Have you not heard anything I've been saying?"

My eyes bulged and I stumbled back from the tabby cat before me. I attempted to point a shaking finger at him. The voice was from Rusty!

Crawling toward the orange cat, I started to poke and prod him. Was there a device on him like a speaker, through which someone else was talking? Was someone playing a prank?

"Stop poking this instant!" The voice spoke again as Rusty's paw reached out to swipe at me.

My investigation paused. Then I did another once-over of Rusty, this time without touching him. There was no device anywhere on him. There was only a cat and me.

"Told you she wasn't the brightest," said a different voice.

This time the voice came from behind me, causing me to take shaky breaths as my eyebrow raised. I turned around slowly, and the only figure that was close by was Luna. There was no way she was speaking as well. Right?

"Luna?" My voice quivered as I spoke, afraid of what might happen next.

"See? Not the brightest one around."

My body froze at her words but I was soon trying to scramble back, dazed at everything that was unfolding. But in my confusion I scrambled away from the cats and slammed into the door. Pain coursed through my body once more as my vision faded and I fell forward. Luna's words drifted through my darkening mind as I fell.

"Here we go again..."

Chapter Five

It must have been several more hours before I regained consciousness. It was dark outside, with no trace of sunlight. The only light that shined was coming from the moon. The events of the day were heavy on my mind, and even though I'd just woken up, I knew everything that had happened hadn't been a dream. It was too bizarre and there was just no way this could have been conjured up.

I headed into the living room after picking myself up off the ground and closing the door that had been left open when I fainted. On my couch were Zaira, Luna, and most importantly, Rusty.

"I see you made yourself comfortable." Sarcasm dripped from my lips as I spoke to the orange cat before me.

"The door was open."

"Look Rusty, I like you. You being able to talk is freaky, but I like you. I just can't have four cats."

"Three."

"I don't think being electrocuted and fainting twice caused me to forget how to count."

"There are only three cats here."

"He is correct," Luna said, agreeing with the orange cat she sat next to. If there were only three cats here then all three were on the couch, where was the fourth one?

"And Lola is where?" I questioned.

"Obviously not here."

I was not becoming a fan of having talking cats around. A quick search of the rest of the house confirmed that the cats were correct. Lola was indeed nowhere to be found. She must have escaped when the door was open, paying no mind to the almost-dead human passed out in the doorway.

I could feel my skin getting flushed and I started to sweat. The cats must have also picked up on my panicked state because Rusty spoke up again from his relaxed position on the couch.

"Great. You are finally understanding."

"This is bad! This is really bad!"

"Right, human. I can tell you where the missing one is."

I crumbled to my knees in front of Rusty. I practically begged for him to tell me where Lola had gone. Because if I didn't find her, I had no idea how I would break the news to my friend that I had already lost one of her cats!

"This information isn't free," Rusty murmured, and then began licking the fur on his paws. The scene between Rusty and me was eerily resembling a scene in a mob movie, with Rusty as the mob boss, and me as the person begging for a second chance and not to get killed.

"And how will I know you will help me locate Lola? Not sure if I can trust talking cats."

"Would I lie? We are human's best friend."

"I'm pretty sure dogs are human's best friend. I would also be willing to bet there is less chance of a dog lying than a cat."

"Do you want my help or not? The way I see it is we either help each other or be both end up not getting what we want."

"Okay, Rusty. Whatever you want, just help me locate Lola."

Rusty perked up and stood. "Great! You have a murder to solve! But first, where is dinner?"

"Excuse me?"

He jumped off the couch and padded over to the food bowl set out for the cats. Remnants of dry food from this morning's meal were still scattered in the bowl.

"This is not acceptable. I require wet food."

"Right. Can we just rewind and go back to the murder part?"

"What do you not understand now? Am I speaking in another language?"

I looked at Rusty in puzzlement. I still couldn't believe a cat was talking to me. If considering the fact that before tonight, having a full-blown conversation could only be a pipe dream. Somebody else's dream—not mine though. I didn't want the ability to talk to cats.

I could tell Rusty was getting frustrated because his tail quivered. He must have always had an early dinnertime with Mrs. Hastings. Hunger could definitely make someone cranky. Or having your owner get murdered could also do it. Either was a good excuse to be frustrated.

"Wait, murder? Mrs. Hastings was murdered?"

"Of course she was! Did you think she just fell over and died?"

I didn't want to answer Rusty because I was really hoping Mrs. Hastings had died of a natural cause, despite what Mrs. Higgins had told me earlier. But it seemed Mrs. Higgins might be onto something like always—murder was at play.

"The food, human!"

I got to my feet and opened the cabinet that contained the cat supplies and I grabbed a can. The second I cracked it open, Luna and Zaira came running to the bowl as well. I stood back and watched them eat after dumping the contents of the can into the bowl.

I couldn't help but think about everything that had happened today. Mrs. Hastings had died, I got electrocuted and also fainted, talking cats were a thing, one cat had escaped, and now I was solving a murder.

"Not bad, but it could be better." Rusty spoke in between consuming his food.

I ignored his comment, already knowing for a fact that Mrs. Hastings had spoiled him.

"I think I should go to sleep. It has been a long day."

"What about the murder?"

"It can wait till the morning; she isn't going anywhere." It was my lame attempt at a joke—I was trying to put some humor in this crazy day in hopes of making the day feel a little bit more normal.

But it was lost on the cats as they just looked at me. I guess my humor was one sided. With nothing else to talk about, I headed to my bedroom to get some well-deserved rest, despite having been knocked unconscious for the majority of the day. This time I would be sleeping of my own free will and not forced into unconsciousness. And hopefully I would be waking up in the morning not having spent the night dreaming of talking cats.

Chapter Six

A buzzing noise slammed into my dreams, disrupting the wonderful scene that had been playing out. It was an odd sensation. One minute I was at an all-you-can-eat buffet of sweets, and next there was an unbearably loud ringing noise. The obnoxious sound continued, and I realized it had to be my phone.

My eyes were still closed as I reached out and grasped my phone. I connected the call and let out a groggy "Hello," as I brought it close to my face. Hopefully, it was someone I could get rid of easily so I could go back to sleep.

"Good morning!"

My eyes shot open as my friend's words filtered through the phone. The same friend for whom I was supposed to be watching and keeping her cats safe. But as of last night, I had lost one.

"How are the cats doing? Any issues?"

My heart raced. How could I tell her I'd lost her cat?

"Good," I said. "They are just being regular cats, you know."

"Can I see them?"

Uh oh.

Not the thing I wanted to hear.

"Can we do this another time? There was some crazy stuff happening yesterday and I'm just really tired."

Her face morphed into one of worry in response as if she were trying to see if I was okay and if I needed to talk. What I really needed was to find Lola. I assured my friend that I was okay and would call soon, then disconnected the call and headed to the living room.

Both Luna and Rusty lounged on the sofa. Zaira was nowhere to be seen, but I knew she didn't have a way to leave the house, so she was just hiding somewhere.

"All right, so there has been a murder. What's next?" I asked the orange cat.

"I don't know. Isn't it *your* job to solve the case?"

"Okay then...what can you tell me about what happened leading up to Mrs. Hastings's sudden death?"

"Well, she was having one of those brunches she always has. Quite a few people showed up."

I nodded. Mrs. Hastings held Sunday brunches at her house very often. It was almost a regular weekly thing. It was also one of the main places Mrs. Higgins got her gossip. After all, gathering a group of nosy old ladies together always resulted in some type of gossip being shared.

"So it's safe to assume that her keeling over didn't happen during the brunch, because Mrs. Higgins would have said something when I talked to her."

"Correct. She died after the brunch gathering."

"And you didn't see anyone whack her?"

"No, we were alone. She was standing one moment and lying on the ground the next moment."

"Okay. Was anyone suspicious around?"

"All humans are suspicious."

Rusty seemed to have lost interest in answering my questions as he walked off and out of my sight, leaving me alone with Luna. Well, if Rusty couldn't answer my questions, maybe Luna could?

"Who do you think did it?"

"I do not know."

My face scrunched at Luna's reply. She was no help. This murder needed to get solved as soon as possible so I could find Lola. Picking up my cell, I called the main number for the police. Maybe they had clues about what happened to Mrs. Hastings, and better yet, maybe they'd already solved the case. If so, I could just skip forward to the part of getting Lola back home safe.

But only a few minutes into the call, I knew the police weren't going to be any help. They did not disclose any new information because it was still open and being reviewed. What was I thinking! The only thing I got was the same information Mrs. Higgins provided.

As of now, it looked like it was a natural cause of death, but they were reviewing everything to make sure no foul play was at hand. After hanging up the phone, I let my body sink into the sofa. I needed to come with my own plan in order to solve this murder and find Lola.

First, I would need to gather clues to find possible suspects for the murder. The second thing would be to actually solve the murder and locate Lola. Third, I would reward myself with a nap because all of this was crazy.

With an action plan now formed, I got up and got to work. First, gather clues, and in order to gather clues, I had to go to the scene of the crime.

A quick kiss on Luna's head and a shout goodbye to Zaira and Rusty, and I made my way across the street. It seemed I was not the only one who had this idea, as Mrs. Hastings's yard was abuzz with activity. A few of the same people who had gathered when the emergency services arrived were here again, this time to pay their respects. And of course, I could spot the curly gray hair of Mrs. Higgins anywhere.

"Mrs. Higgins! How are you today?"

"Better than Rose." Her reply caught me off guard.

It might have been a little too soon to make a joke,

but Mrs. Higgins did what Mrs. Higgins wanted, no matter the time or place.

"Who is handling Mrs. Hastings' items?"

"Her son has been in town for a while, so he is handling things."

"Oh? Zack is in town?"

I hadn't known that. Rose didn't have a husband anymore, and she only had one child, which was Zack. He spent most of the time traveling for work and barely stopped by to visit his mother. He was a few years older than me and had a very successful career, so it made sense he was too busy to come to this quiet town where nothing exciting ever happened.

"Yes, he was way overdue for a visit."

I headed inside after thanking Mrs. Higgins for her information. There were several of the neighbors mingling about in the home, no doubt gossiping and not being mindful that it had only been a day since Mrs. Hastings' death.

In the living room, I found Zack. He was just staring out the window, lost in thought. He looked pained, and I was sure he was still trying to process the events of yesterday.

"Good afternoon, Zack," I softly called out to him as I sat on the second couch.

"Afternoon, Kat. How are you?"

"I'm okay, but *how are you*?"

He turned to me, finally letting his eyes drift from the window.

"I'll be better."

I gave Zack a small smile as I got back up from the couch. I could tell he was not in a talkative mood and I wouldn't force him to be in one. Instead, it would be a good time to search the home for clues.

Chapter Seven

It was time to snoop around the house. But how did one look for clues when one had no idea what to look for? I couldn't linger in the living room much longer and snooping with Zack in the room was just downright awkward. So the living room would have to be the last place I looked. Hopefully by then, Zack would be busy doing something else.

I had been to the Hastings's home a few times, but it was mostly to attend one of the many brunches held here. But those gatherings usually always took place outside in the garden. Since that was the most familiar area to me, I decided the garden should be the first place I looked. My body weaved between the people walking about the house before I managed to make it outside.

It honestly looked just like any other time I'd been there, but I also knew a clue wouldn't just be sitting in plain sight. No matter how much I really wanted it to be so, this case wouldn't be over and done with that easily.

The garden had a simple setup. Mrs. Hastings did not have a huge home, as she preferred to spend most of her time outdoors, which meant she made sure to keep her garden area looking beautiful with a variety of colorful flowers and simple seating. White wrought-iron furniture was scattered throughout the backyard in a tasteful manner. A table with two chair setup was placed in several spots in the garden which allowed people to sit in different parts of the garden. In the center of the garden a medium-size outdoor couch with several chairs surrounded a table. That was the common place people gathered during most of the parties held here.

The table and chairs off to the side of the garden was actually my favorite spot to sit. Often times, it was a bit awkward at the main table. I felt like I wasn't old enough to be at the grownup table. It also seemed that several ladies, especially Mrs. Higgins, took a special interest in my personal life as they probed for information to keep their gossip ring alive.

I inspected each seating setup as I maneuvered around the garden. Nothing seemed out of the ordinary—not even the flowers around the furniture and along the walkway. Everything was perfectly in place and tidy, which would have been odd if this had been anyone's house but Mrs. Hastings's. For the frequent number of gatherings held here at her home, she was known to keep her home super tidy. One could never be too prepared for guests.

This seemed to confirm what Rusty had stated—that Mrs. Hastings did not succumb to death during the brunch, but after. She'd had enough time to clean up after her guests, so it had to have been at least a few hours after the party before she arrived at death's door. With one final look around the garden and nodding my approval that it was a lost cause and no clues could be found here, I headed back inside.

Upon walking into the home, I knew the next stop to search for clues would be the bathroom. With the bathroom as my next target, it would be easy to search as it allowed for one occupant at a time. As I headed that way, I bumped right into Mrs. Higgins, who was leaving the restroom.

"Kat, we really have to stop meeting like this." She laughed as she passed me, allowing me entrance to the restroom.

I nodded my head in agreement as I continued pushing forward to enter the room. I closed the door as I shot a smile in Mrs. Higgins direction.

With a sigh of relief, I turned to the mirror. I was a bit hesitant to talk to Mrs. Higgins for fear I would let loose the information that I was looking for clues. No doubt Mrs. Higgins would help me look for clues, but there would be no way I could tell her that I was only doing this because a talking cat had told me to. She didn't think I was crazy, but after that tidbit of information, I was sure she would definitely think I was losing my sanity.

That was something that could not happen until Lola was back home, safe and sound. I could not be sent off and locked away until I knew my friend's cat was okay.

The first thing that drew my attention as a place that might possibly hold some clues was the medicine cabinet. I popped it open and inside there were three shelves. They weren't overflowing with items—Mrs. Hastings actually didn't have too many things in her cabinet. Most of them were vitamins and over-the-counter medicines. Nothing alarming about those items. After inspecting the cabinets and moving a few objects around, nothing looked to be prescribed. So Mrs. Hastings was definitely in good health, and it was beginning to look more like murder as time passed.

There was also a cup with a single toothbrush in the cabinet. If there was another toothbrush, I would have had a clue that there was somebody in her life, but with a single toothbrush there was no one else to consider. Other than that, the contents of the cabinet were standard. Nothing screamed murder weapon.

With the medicine cabinet investigated, I crouched down to search underneath the sink. Just like the cabinet, there wasn't anything underneath that was grabbing my attention in a way that suggested it could have been involved with the murder. Just supplies for restocking, like toilet paper, towels, and hand soap. Nothing alarming in the cabinet. I closed the doors and leaned against the counter, allowing myself to rest for a moment.

"What am I doing?" I whispered to myself. I was in way over my head. I didn't know the first thing to look for in a case like this.

Why was I even trying to solve this case? All the movies made it seem like evidence with blood on it would always be present. But here? Everything was perfectly clean and in order, which also happened to be completely normal for Mrs. Hastings. This case was an impossible case.

With a deep breath to collect my thoughts, I leaned forward to inspect the bathtub. Just a few bottles of shampoo, conditioner, and body wash. Again, everything was normal and nothing looked odd or gave off vibes that it was involved with the murder.

Maybe the drain? I inspected the drain to see if I could locate any strands of hair of another color, but again it was spotless. Not even a single strand of Mrs. Hastings's hair was sticking out!

Letting out a huff at another dead end, I wondered if things displayed in movies were even accurate at all. Drains always seemed like an important clue in almost every detective show. Well, the movies couldn't always be right, it seemed.

Just for good measure, I turned to the toilet and popped off the top. I drew back slightly with a grimace at the hint of smell that lifted, but again there was nothing there. Normally in the movies, people would hide some money here even possibly the murder weapon, but other than a tingle of a smell, nothing was being hidden here. As I attempted to put the lid back on, several knocks echoed throughout the restroom and I froze.

This was not a good position to be in because there were only two things to say if I got caught with the toilet top off. Either I was looking for clues, or I clogged the toilet so badly I was inspecting it. And I wasn't sure which answer would actually be worse to admit to.

"Just a minute!" I called out.

Somehow managing to flip faucet for the sink to turn on to create some white noise, I was finally able to get the tank lid back on. Thankfully, the running water did help to muffle some of the noise of the lid sliding back into place.

With the water already running, I allowed myself a moment to wash my hands and collect my thoughts. I opened the door to be greeted by another neighbor, who only gave me a quick smile before proceeding into the bathroom while ushering me out. Guess his business couldn't wait.

With the backyard and bathroom scoped out and cleared, I needed to find another room to search for clues. I eyed Mrs. Hastings' bedroom, but doubted I could efficiently search her room with so many guests present. If I got caught in her room, it would definitely raise a few eyebrows. And if I felt rushed and went too quickly, I might miss something important.

With the bedroom knocked to the bottom of the list, along with the living room, I headed to the kitchen. The most crowded room of the house. It seemed no matter the occasion, people would always flock around the food.

Chapter Eight

The kitchen was crowded but luckily it contained fewer people than when I had first entered the home. Off in the corner sitting at the dining room table was Mrs. Higgins, drinking a cup of tea. A few other ladies from the neighborhood sat around her at the table, and together they formed their gossip ring. Not wanting to stare at her too long in case she thought I wanted to join them, I headed to the island in the middle of the kitchen.

After browsing the selection of food, I settled on a few pieces of dessert. Namely a cheesecake with a raspberry sauce and a few snickerdoodle cookies. I stuffed a piece of cheesecake in my mouth and began my investigation in a room full of people, doing my best to not make it obvious that I was looking for clues. I opened and peered inside a few of the cabinets, trying to find anything that stood out. One cabinet contained fancy china which I was sure rarely got used. The next one contained a whole collection of mismatched cups but again nothing stood out as noteworthy and certainly nothing screamed murder.

It was opening the third cabinet that got someone's attention, and a light tapping on my shoulder caused me to turn around.

"What are you doing?"

Having run into Mrs. Higgins only meant sooner or later I would run into Mr. Higgins. And if I had my choice, I would take Mrs. over Mr. anytime.

Somehow, I was able to plaster a smile on my face as I gave the man who was slightly shorter than I a reply.

"Searching."

It wasn't a lie, just some information was omitted. After all I couldn't directly blurt out that I was looking for a murder weapon in a room where anybody could be the killer.

I could tell he was waiting for me to elaborate on my answer. But when I did not, his eyebrow arched and he leveled a look at me that made it seem like I'd gotten caught with my hand in the cookie jar. Which technically, I had.

"And what pray tell are you searching for?" he quizzed.

My eyes stayed trained on the imposing figure in front of me while my mind raced through a thousand possible responses. Being a retired detective could have that impact. I needed a reply that would not make me look guilty. The only things my thoughts revolved around were murder and food.

I couldn't confess to searching for evidence of murder, so my only option was food. The raspberry cheesecake was really good, but I couldn't say I was searching for that in the cabinets. But I could say I was searching for the sauce!

With the half-eaten cheesecake with raspberry sauce still on my plate, I thrusted it forward toward Mr. Higgins to show him my slice. While also including a smile on my face, I provided an Oscar-worthy response.

"This cheesecake is to die for! I wanted to find out what sauce was used, so I could make it at home." I omitted the fact that I didn't have any plans to create a cheesecake anytime soon.

Mr. Higgins' face morphed into a smile as my own morphed into a frown of bewilderment. Why was he smiling?

He patted the air a little indicating I should lean in a fraction. I answered his request by tilting my head down a portion to get closer. He cast his eyes around for a few before he leaned in and whispered in my ear.

"It's actually my secret recipe."

I couldn't help but look at the guy facing me in confusion. My eyebrows knitted together at his statement while the smile on his face grew even bigger.

"It's a family recipe. But come on over anytime and I will give you some to take home."

"Oh wow, I appreciate that."

"So you can stop checking the cabinets, because you will never find it there." He laughed as he waved goodbye and made his way out of the kitchen.

Well, now it would be awkward if I kept searching after Mr. Higgins just told me to stop. With the kitchen no longer searchable, it was time to head to the next room on the list.

But before continuing the search, one must stock back up on food. After all, one did not think clearly when hunger was present.

I wasn't sure if the gnawing in my stomach was from actually being hungry, or from being nervous. Everything I was doing was ridiculous and far outside my comfort zone. I had been just seconds away from getting caught by an ex-cop!

Maybe there was something else on the kitchen island that looked appetizing and could help settle my nerves. My eyes stopped on the mac and cheese. I took the spoon and plopped a lump onto my plate. Probably a horrible idea to eat mac and cheese after sweets, but considering that this whole day was a horrible idea, it fit perfectly.

"Not going for more of the cheesecake?"

My body tensed at the words. Of course it would be my luck to get away from Mr. Higgins only to run into the Mrs. once more. Turning to the lady that had sneaked up on me, I gave her a smile. It seemed like I was giving a lot of forced smiles today.

"Thought I should try some other things as well." I muttered.

"Good, no reason to give that man a bigger ego than he already has. I heard you like the sauce." Mrs. Higgins went to work at the island filling, a few plates with food.

"Yes, very much."

"Good, he told you could stop by anytime, right?"

"Yes, he sure did."

"Great! Help me carry this over to the table."

She shoved a plate in my direction, forcing me to grab it along with my own. With two plates of food in her own hands she headed to the table where the gossip ring ladies sat.

After placing the plates on the table, Mrs. Higgins slid back into her seat. She patted the seat next to her, indicating I should sit down as well, but I was there on a mission and couldn't waste time getting caught up in the latest scandal.

"Sorry, I'll join another time," I blurted out while setting the plate handed to me earlier on the table.

Before I could withdraw my arm and make an escape, Paula Gibbs, the most entitled lady on the block, grabbed it.

"Join us. You young people always act like you are busy but really, do you have anything going on? You spend a lot of time at home alone anyways."

I cleared my throat as I got ready to give her a piece of my mind, but Mrs. Higgins beat me to it and spoke up for me.

"Paula, if she doesn't want to join us, she doesn't need to."

"Well obviously she doesn't need to. One should respect their elders and humor their request though, right?"

"Kat, spend five minutes with us and that will shut Paula up and then you can go. It will save us all from listening to her complain for the next hour if you don't."

"That's quite rude to say to a friend, April."

"Friend is a loose term here," Mrs. Higgins bit back.

A few chuckles escaped from my lips. I couldn't contain them as they verbally jabbed each other. Mrs. Gibbs sent me a glare but my chuckles continued. I slid into the seat next to Mrs. Higgins, placing my own plate before me on the table.

The gossip ring continued on with their conversation like the last few seconds hadn't happened. I could only hope that when I aged, I would be more like April Higgins than Paula Gibbs.

"I can't believe Rose was the first to go," Paula said as she wiped invisible tears from her face. Her short black hair bobbed with her movement but did nothing to conceal the fact she was indeed not crying.

"Oh stuff it, Paula. No reason to be fake when everyone here already knows."

"Goodness April, you don't have a single nice bone in your body, do you?"

"Says the lady that complains every month because she loses the best lawn contest." Another sharp reply from Mrs. Higgins. who was turning out to be the most amazing lady ever.

"Well can you blame me? My lawn is ten times better than Rose's. I honestly don't know how she ended up winning all the time." Paula picked up her cup of tea and brought it to her lips to take a sip.

While everyone took a moment to let Paula have her say, I scanned the rest of the table, taking in who else was present. At the table also sat Fiona West and Sharon Smith. There were others in the so-called gossip ring, but they had either left the gathering or were out of town, causing them not to be present.

Fiona was the quietest of the group. She was the quiet one who was always present, but she rarely offered a piece of her mind; usually she just stated facts.

Fiona West had long, black hair that went to her butt and was always in a braid of some kind. Today her hair was split—the top half was pulled back and braided, laying on top of the bottom half of her hair, which had been left free. Higgins was my favorite on the block, but West would be a close second.

The final person at the gossip ring table was Sharon Smith. She was like April, with her outspoken opinions. But it was usually only on certain topics. Her fiery red curly hair made a statement and allowed her to stand out. I often doubted her hair was actually that naturally vibrant, but she claimed it was all natural. Sharon was the wild one of the group. If there was some type of scandal it usually could always be traced back to Sharon in some way. But as a never-married woman with no kids, she had the luxury of being completely wild and not caring what others thought of her as it didn't have an impact on anyone but herself. She insisted on always being called by her first name because using her last name made her feel old.

"I don't understand what is so important about having the best lawn," Sharon piped in. She picked at the food on her plate, trying to find something to snack on.

"It's not something we would think you would understand. Priorities and all."

That comment caused Sharon to stop poking around at the food and level a glare at Mrs. Gibbs.

"Well, sorry for not being the typically old bat of a lady like yourself."

"Excuse me? What did you say?"

"Ladies, ladies, calm down. We are here for Rose, and not to hear you squabble." Right on cue, Mrs. Higgins injected words of wisdom.

But I knew things weren't going to calm down anytime soon. They were probably just getting started, if the red tint increasing on Sharon's cheeks was any indication. Any minute now and it would match the flaming hair on her head.

"I think that is my signal to leave," I said as I rose from my chair. Both Mrs. Higgins and Mrs. West waved goodbye while the verbal fighting match between Mrs. Gibbs and Sharon escalated and caused heads to turn in their direction.

Chapter Nine

The day's events left me drained and exhausted. My mind reeled from a hundred thoughts, trying to process if today had been fruitful in gaining clues or if it was just a waste of time.

With remote in hand, I lounged on the couch and relaxed as I clicked through the channels. I tried to find something to watch, but nothing was grabbing my interest as it seemed my mind was in another place. Luna made a noise when I landed on the food channel.

"Want to watch this?"

"I would prefer if you gave me actual food," Luna piped up from her position on my stomach.

As I rubbed my hands along her back while also giving her chin scratches, the sounds of her purring increased. I decided to humor the little feline and let her watch food on tv, so I left it on that channel.

"Is Rusty still here?" I asked.

"Yeah, he's being a lazy one."

Rusty's claws lightly echoed in the home as he made his way over to the living room, sensing us talking about him.

"Solve the case yet?"

Luna slid from my stomach to my lap as I sat up.

"Not even close. I have no idea what I am doing. Are you sure you don't know who did it?" I replied to the orange cat.

"If I knew who did it, do you think I would waste my time here in this measly home?"

That comment irked me. Yes, my home wasn't fancy, with expensive items and rare china on display like Mrs. Hastings had. But home was home, and it was comfy.

"Honestly, in order for this to work don't you think we should handle this together?"

Rusty jumped up on the couch next to my side and proceeded to make himself comfortable. He invaded my space like we were best friends, not bothering with the fact that two seconds ago, he had insulted me.

"What do you need from me?" he asked.

"Well, was anything different on the day of her death? Did you see anything out of the ordinary? Maybe someone new or perhaps they were acting weird?"

"I don't know."

"What do you mean you don't know? Were you asleep the whole time?"

"No. I was locked in the bedroom for the party and was let out once everyone left."

"Is that what usually happens?"

"Hmm...No. But I didn't mind because she gave me lots of treats."

Rusty purred, most likely thinking about the fancy treats he had gotten for being locked in the room for the party. In order to get Rusty's attention back on track, I leaned in closer before continuing my line of questioning.

"Did Mrs. Hasting say why she locked you in the room?"

Rusty tilted his head from side to side as if that motion would drag the memory back into his mind.

"Something about I would make someone sneeze. But how would I do that? I'm not dirty!"

The gears in my mind turned as I took in everything Rusty was saying. He was usually allowed to attend Mrs. Hastings's brunches, except for the last one. After which Rose Hastings ended up dead, but not dead during or right after, because she'd had time to clean up from the gathering and let Rusty out of the room.

If Rusty was going to make someone sneeze, then someone at the party was probably allergic to cats. The biggest clue of all was that this person did not attend brunches often, or Rusty would have made comments that he was often locked in the bedroom. But this had been a one-off.

A smile started to spread on my face because it seemed that I'd solved the mystery. Well maybe not solved it, but this revelation sure brought me one step closer. The person who killed Rose Hastings did not like being around cats and unlucky for that person, I was surrounded by them. I could use them to sniff the person out—all I had to do was let them loose on the neighbors.

Maybe being a detective wouldn't be so hard after all, especially if one had talking cats for assistants.

After moving Luna off my lap and onto the couch next to Rusty, I jumped to my feet. Now all I needed to know was who had attended the party, and I knew just the person who would have that information. Mrs. Higgins of course.

"Found a clue?" Luna asked from her new spot on the couch.

"Sure did!"

"Well leave the TV on, I'm enjoying this show."

"It would be better if she just fed us," Rusty added, sharing his own two cents.

"Exactly what I said." Luna spoke.

The cats kept discussing their lack of dinner, despite it not being time for dinner. I paid them no mind as I slipped on my shoes and made my way outside. Instead of going across the street to Mrs. Hastings' home, I headed to the right to the Higgins' home.

Knocking on the front door, I was greeted by Mr.

Higgins already dressed in his pajamas, even though just two hours ago he had been fully dressed and at Mrs. Hastings's home.

"Kat, what can I do for you?" he asked as his eyebrow raised a little at my sudden appearance at their home.

"I was wondering if I could have some of that raspberry sauce."

His face brightened at my words and he motioned me in. I crossed the threshold into their home and he wasted no time in closing the door behind me.

"Couldn't last a day without more, eh?" He laughed as he headed to the kitchen and I followed behind.

Upon entering the kitchen, I found Mrs. Higgins sitting on the bench at the dining table, looking outside into their backyard through the glass French doors.

"Look who couldn't wait a second longer to get their hands on my secret sauce."

"Timothy, the sauce really isn't that great," Mrs. Higgins stated while sipping on a cup of tea.

Mr. Higgins shot a smile in my direction before sending a glare over to his wife. "At least someone has good taste, isn't that right Kat?"

I knew better to make a comment. Because I knew for a fact it was Mrs. Higgins who did most of the cooking and I would rather be on her good side than on Mr. Higgins's when it came to food.

Pulling out a chair to sit at the opposite end of the

table to Mrs. Higgins, I took the teapot on the table and poured myself a cup of tea.

I instantly noticed that there were two cups on the table, and Mrs. Higgins already had one, so there had been three total. Almost like they had been expecting company. Had they known I was coming over? Mrs. Higgins seemed to have read my mind, as she stopped looking outside and sent a smile my way.

"So did you really come over for his sauce or was it something else?" she asked. Nothing seemed to escape the eye of Mrs. Higgins after all.

"What gave me away?"

"Searching the cabinets in another person's home while the room is full? Dear, you should watch some more mystery shows." She laughed as a look of embarrassment spread across my face. I couldn't tell her that I was looking into the murder because a cat had asked me to. That was not something I was ready to explain, or even had the ability to explain, as it seemed I was the only one who could understand cat language.

"Are you looking into her death too?"

"Heavens no! I promised Timothy I would stop meddling in people's affairs. He gets so worried when I get put in danger."

"Danger, in this town?"

Mrs. Higgins's eyes lit up and seemed to smile at me as she brought her cup to her lips and sipped.

"Not everything is as it seems all the time,

especially in this cozy town of ours," she said after a few sips. "But Timothy did not forbid me from helping someone who asks for my help. Granted, he couldn't have known someone would be asking for my help." She giggled while setting down her cup of tea. "So. What questions do you have for me?" she continued.

"I was wondering if you could tell me who was at the brunch."

"Good place to start. Got to know your suspects in order to make an informed decision about who committed the crime."

Taking a moment to pause, she then continued speaking. "This one was a lively one, almost like Rose knew it was her last hurrah."

Mrs. Higgins grabbed the teapot in front of me and refilled our cups before setting it back down. It seemed like I would be here for a while.

"You asked who was at the party, so let me think for a moment. There was Rose Hastings, Bridget Tanner, Paula Gibbs, Fiona West, Sharon Smith, Lucy Walker, Alec Ford, and finally myself."

"Wow, that is quite a list. Even though you attended I think we can knock you off the list."

"Are you positive?"

I could see the smirk growing on Mrs. Higgins' face at her words.

"I doubt you would have killed Rose Hastings and then mention you thought she got murdered." I laughed out loud.

"Ah, but you should never factor someone out unless you are one hundred percent sure they are innocent."

I had no doubt in my mind that Mrs. Higgins was not the murderer, because why would she provide me with so many clues? Despite her saying not to mark her off the list, I did. But I continued to listen as she told me the events of the brunch.

Chapter Ten

With a can of gravy-style, wet cat food in hand, I proceed to the kitchen. Three small bowls had already been set out on the counter, making it easier for me as I started to portion the food out. Luna instantly came running into the kitchen, quickly followed by Zaira and Rusty. The sight of Rusty caused me to pause, because it should have been Lola running in to get her food instead.

I set the three bowls down on the ground before standing back and letting them dive in.

"I have a list of names of those who were at the brunch," I said to the cats while they carried on eating. They paid no attention to me, so I continued to speak. "I can knock one off the list because there is just no way she did it. Another can be knocked off the list because she's dead. Which leaves a suspect pool of six."

The beep from the microwave indicated that my own dinner was done heating up. With my plate in hand, along with my spoon, I sat down at the dining table. Luna finished her food quickly and jumped on the dining table to join me—no doubt waiting to see if I would feed her some of my human food.

"Any of them seem like the murderer?" she asked.

"I'm not sure. I just know the person is allergic to cats. But I have the perfect plan to figure out who committed the crime," I responded with my mouth full of food.

"And let me guess, that involves one of us?"

She was smart. I nodded as I continued to eat.

"Of course. Best way to figure out if someone is allergic to cats is to introduce them to cats."

"I figured. Well, don't sign me up," Luna muttered as she left to another room in the home.

Which left me with the two remaining cats, who were currently finishing the last of their food. Zaira's body tensed when she felt my eyes on her.

"What about you Zaira? Will you help me?"

She looked at me for a moment before hightailing it out of sight.

"Great conversation. What about you Rusty?"

"What about me?"

"Have you not been listening?"

Rusty didn't reply, but instead he started to lick his paw. With another mouthful of food stuffed in my mouth, I sat in silence waiting for him to provide a reply. But it seemed the orange cat was intent on ignoring me.

"Well, in order to solve the case I need a cat. Don't you want me to solve the case?"

"I guess. But what exactly do you need from me?"

"Nothing really, I just need to go around talking to all the neighbors to see which one doesn't want to be near you."

"Everyone wants to be near me." he replied snarkily.

"Everyone but the murderer."

"Fine. Hurry up human, we've got a case to solve. I can't wait around all day for you."

"Oh, now you actually want to do things? You'll just have to wait a few minutes, until I've finished eating."

"What about when I wanted food before you left the house earlier?"

Rusty was the definition of dramatic, and I knew he was attempting to rile me up to get more food. Instead, I continued eating. A list of six suspects wasn't very long, but it was still a decent amount of people to wade through.

I also couldn't help but think that someone on that list had murdered Rose Hastings and I was in the process of sniffing them out. I hoped whatever they did to bring Mrs. Hastings to an early grave didn't happen to me too—because solving this case wasn't even something I wanted to do.

I continued thinking about what would happen

next as I shoved a few more bites of food into my mouth. Rusty and I would have to go door-to-door and see who reacted to the orange cat, who had no problem speaking his mind. Hopefully everyone would be home, and we wouldn't have to track anyone down.

"Finally!" A frustrated meow left his mouth as I got up to put my bowl in the sink.

"Yes, yes. I'm done. Let's go."

Rusty jumped off the table and headed toward the front door. My hand grasped the doorknob, and I yanked it open to head outside with the orange cat a few steps behind me. Against all better judgement, we left the safety of my home to go sniff out a murderer.

Chapter Eleven

I stared up into the dark eyes of Paula Gibbs, who looked at me like I interrupted her spa treatment —which might have been true because she did answer in a bathrobe and her hair wrapped up in a towel.

"Kat, you interrupted my personal time. Why are you here?"

"Sorry to bother you, but I wanted to know if you know what will happen to Rusty now that Mrs. Hastings is gone?" I asked her. My hands lightly gripped Rusty's stomach, and I thrust him forward into her face.

"Really? You couldn't have asked this earlier?"

I peered at her around the orange coat of the cat I was holding in front of me. She didn't move backward as if the cat was cursed and was about to bring forward a fury of sneezes. Instead, she just looked even more annoyed that I was asking about a *cat*, of all things.

"Please Kat. Go bother someone else. I don't want the orange cat. He eats too much." With those parting words she slammed the door in my face.

Rusty's job was complete, so I lowered him back down to the ground and let him go.

"I think that went well." I muttered. With another name crossed off the list, that just left five names now.

"I'm not fat." The angry huff from Rusty broke through the silence.

Bending down for a second to give him a pat, I headed on to the next house. One of the next-door neighbors of Mrs. Gibbs was the Tanner family. Mrs. Higgins had said Bridget attended the brunch, which was odd, since Bridget was a few years younger than me and avoided the gossip ring like the plague—because if they weren't talking about Sharon Smith, they were surely talking about Bridget Tanner.

My knuckles knocked against the door of the pearl-colored home I did not have to wait long to be greeted by the sight of Bridget Tanner. She crossed her arms and leaned against the door. Her wavy blonde hair was a bit of a mess and she wore a crop top and sweatpants.

"Kat, what's up?" she asked, totally looking uninterested that I was at her front door.

"You attended the brunch at Mrs. Hastings' house the day she died?"

That got her attention. Bridget stood up a bit straighter, like she was now very interested in the conversation and my presence.

"Freaky, right? I didn't know she was just going to kick the bucket. If so, I would have stuck around. I haven't seen a dead body before."

I stared at Bridget. We were friends at one point but her habit of sneaking out past our curfew when we were younger and the weird and crazy stuff that she somehow got herself into eventually caused me to cut ties. But at least some things did not change—Bridget would always be Bridget.

"I didn't take you to be the type to hang out with the gossip ring."

Bridget let out a laugh at the nickname I'd given the crew of ladies that joined together almost weekly to dish on everything going on.

"Oh I'm not. But mom gave me $50 to go while she is out of town."

"How long has she been gone?"

"Only a few days. She's supposed to be gone for a week, but when I called about Rose Hastings falling over dead, she was thinking about coming back early."

I nodded my head at her words. Bridget was definitely on the list of suspects. She usually didn't attend the brunch, but she attended the latest one and Rusty was not locked up in the room till this last brunch. Now in order to knock her off the list or secure her spot on it, she needed to pass the cat test.

I gave a little nudge to the orange cat at my side to let him know it was his time to shine. He trotted forward but before doing so he let out a meow at his displeasure at being forced to work. At first, Bridget paid no attention to the cat that brushed in between her legs. Briefly tossing her hair back over her shoulder and behind her ears, she started to pick at her nails.

"Honestly. All this is freaky. Don't you think?"

My eyes darted to Rusty who had now invited himself into her home.

"Why do you say so?" I stomped my foot a little to see if I could grab the attention of the orange cat and get him to come back outside again.

"If anyone was going to die, I would have thought it would be Mrs. Higgins. She can't keep her nose out of anything and if it was me, I would have finished her off first. Get rid of the worst one, right?"

I tried to process her words as I stared at the blonde girl before me. My head tilted to the side as I tried to read the expression on Bridget's face, but she seemed like this was just any other day and just any old conversation between friends.

"Mrs. Higgins is known for information on everyone, so I guess."

"Yeah, maybe they meant to kill Higgins instead of Hastings?"

Now that was a very interesting thing to say. As of now, the only real person who thought it was murder was Mrs. Higgins, but it seemed Bridget also thought it was murder. The real question was why?

"Why do you say that? Did you notice anything the day of the brunch that seemed off?" I questioned.

"I don't know. It was just the vibe, you know? I could feel it in the air."

Well, that was not the information I was wanting to hear from Bridget. It wasn't very helpful and going to the cops stating that "it was the vibe" was evidence they would throw out the window.

"Did the vibe in the air tell you anything else?"

Despite my best effort to hide how funny I found the situation, I still let out a croaking laugh.

"Funny. Laugh all you want, but I'm sure it was murder. That is what I told my mom, and that is why she might come back early. She probably thinks we are all going to end up like Rose Hastings—dead on the living room floor." She paused before continuing. "Well I don't have any plans on being the next one."

Bridget stood a little straighter while she looked at me. "Why did you come over here, anyways? Surely not just to ask me if I attended the brunch?"

"Caught red-handed!" I laughed. "I was actually trying to see if you wanted to take care of Rusty."

"Who is Rusty?" she quizzed back.

I pointed my finger at the orange cat who was currently making himself at home and sniffing some of the random items on the floor of Bridget's living room. Most likely he was trying to determine if any of the items were edible.

Bridget tossed a casual glance over her shoulder

and looked at the orange cat briefly before looking back at me. It was only a second before her face changed to a look of horror and disgust and then she rushed inside to grab Rusty. He let out a squeak at being picked up so roughly. Bridget quickly returned to the door and set him down next to me.

"So, you don't like cats?"

She wasn't sneezing, but maybe Mrs. Hastings just said sneezing because Bridget was always dramatic with everything. I wouldn't have put it past her to say she was going to die from being around cats just so she wouldn't have to be near them.

"I mean, I don't mind if others have cats, but their fur gets everywhere! So I'm not a fan."

Once again, I picked up Rusty and thrust him forward toward Bridget, to just confirm that she wasn't going to sneeze. Instead of recoiling, she reached out and started giving him some chin scratches, causing the orange cat to purr at the attention. Well, that knocked Bridget off the list for Rose's murder. But if Mrs. Higgins ever ended up dead, Bridget would be my prime suspect.

"Thanks for the information, it was great catching up," I called out as I quickly left Bridget's front steps and headed toward my own home with Rusty safely tucked in my arms.

Chapter Twelve

Morning could have taken its sweet time coming, but it snuck up on me and smacked me right in the face. All the cat fur surrounding me might have been a trigger that caused me to wake up early, but I'd never know for sure.

I stumbled out of bed and into the living room after casting Rusty's body off me and onto the bedcovers. There, I curled up on the couch as I flicked the TV on, and it wasn't long before the cats migrated to the couch to join me.

Trying to solve a murder was exhausting and weird. I was forced to start seeing my neighbors in a new light. It would take some getting used to. Hopefully, this would be the one and only murder on the block. If there were any more talking cats and dead bodies, I would gladly check myself into an insane asylum because I would have to be crazy.

"Why are you wasting daylight?" Rusty's first words of the morning broke into my thoughts, causing me to roll my eyes at his behavior.

"Why can't you go to the cops?"

"Because I went to you."

"Yes, but you could have just gone to the cops in the first place."

"You are the only person who seems to understand us."

"Why, because I'm crazy?" I snorted.

"You said it, not me," Rusty said, obviously very pleased that I classified myself as crazy.

"Right," I said. "So on to today's agenda. We still have four people to track down and figure out if they like cats or not, but everyone is going to be at work so it's going to be a bit hard..." I thought about how we could narrow down the list even more.

"Who is first?" Rusty spoke out.

"It doesn't really matter because I don't think I will be able to bring a cat into a workplace with me. So I have to search by myself during work hours."

"Great! I was hoping for the day off!" With those parting words, Rusty jumped off the couch and onto the floor, heading back into my bedroom to reclaim my bed.

I followed Rusty's lead and got off the couch but instead of heading back to my bedroom, I headed toward the kitchen. With some snacks and my keys in hand, it was time to go out and discover who killed Rose Hastings.

"Bye, cats!" I called out to the felines that I was forced to share my home with and headed outside.

The walk to the central district was short, as the town was small. But just because the town was small didn't mean the central district didn't have everything you could ever ask for.

The very first place on my stop was the most popular place to gather—the Sips of Temptation café. I let out a big snort of amusement as a thought popped in my mind. I recalled Mrs. Higgins's opinion on the unique name of the café. The owner of the café was Sharon Smith. She had a notorious reputation of being a social butterfly for all the wrong reasons. She still maintained that free-wheeling lifestyle, talking to whoever she wanted. A true temptation in the city.

Tempting whoever she wanted, no matter the scenario. Which caused a bit of drama with several couples within town. It only made sense that Sharon would name the café to reflect her personality.

The bell above the door rang as I entered. The café wasn't large; but it also wasn't a shoebox size. But what worked in its favor was the millions of windows that let in sunlight all day long, making the place seem bigger than it was. It also helped establish a warm feeling which brought customers through its doors at all hours of the day.

"Good Afternoon, Kat!" called out Ethan from behind the front counter.

"Afternoon," I replied, returning his smile.

"What can I get for you today?" he asked as he rolled up the sleeves of his gray shirt.

The uniforms of the café were a bit more professional looking than the standard café dress. The whole reason the employees looked so professional was to add to the temptation feel. After all, who didn't like someone in a uniform? Along with the gray button-down shirt they all wore black slacks. A very clean look for the café indeed.

"Just an iced coffee for now, please."

Ethan began making my drink while I scanned the room. The majority of tables were taken, except for a few in the back corner. With another glance around to confirm no one present was on my list of suspects, I settled at a two-seater table. I didn't have to wait long till I heard a soft tap on the tabletop, and my cup of iced coffee was pushed toward me.

"Let me know if you need anything else."

"Will do."

Grabbing the cold drink off the table and taking a sip, I let out a sigh of relief. That first sip of coffee always made my body tingle. I relaxed and let myself slouch back into my chair. I stared at the door while sipping away at my drink slowly, just enjoying the quiet time.

Miraculously, I was able to savor my drink for an

hour before it started to taste a bit watered down. An iced coffee was not meant to last that long. But even with keeping the front door in sight the whole time, I still didn't see any sign of Sharon. Could today be one of her rare days off? She was obsessed with the café and spent the majority of her time here, so taking time off was weird.

I could either buy another drink and wait some more, or head out and do something else. I was getting increasingly bored, and my body ached from sitting for so long. I needed to get the blood flowing back through my body so I stretched my legs out in front of me and raised my arms over my head, then followed with a few twists. A murder had to be solved, which meant I was stuck on this stakeout regardless of how much I wanted to go home and be lazy.

I headed back to the front counter and placed another order for an iced coffee. This time I waited up front instead of heading back to my secluded table.

"Bored?"

"My face gave it away?" I chuckled at Ethan's words. Anyone taking a glance my way could tell I was bored out of my mind.

"Just had a feeling. What are you waiting around here for?"

"I need to talk to Sharon."

"Oh, she took the day off. Actually, she will be gone for several days. New boyfriend and everything."

Whenever Sharon found a new love interest, she

did tend to become extremely invested. So she had taken a few days off to enjoy the new love.

"Well, I wish I would have known that earlier."

"What do you need to talk to Sharon about? Are you looking to join us finally here at the café?"

"Never in a million years. I'm just trying to find a home for Rusty, who was Rose Hastings's cat."

"Ah, that orange tabby cat."

"You have met Rusty before?"

"No, but Sharon talks about that cat like it's the bane of her existence."

That puzzled me. If Sharon had multiple run-ins with Rusty then it would make sense that she was not the murderer, as Rusty would have been locked away on more occasions than just the last get-together. But as Mrs. Higgins had said, *don't mark someone off the list until you are completely sure they are not the murderer*.

"Why doesn't she like him? He seems okay, even though he seems posh."

"Supposedly, Mrs. Hastings got really sick one time years ago, and she needed someone to care for Rusty. Sharon ended up getting bribed into doing it since she lives alone, and let's just say, Sharon had to buy some new furniture after she watched that cat."

Even though I tried to contain it, a chuckle left my lips. Rusty, and even Luna, were very expressive when it came to their food, and I had no doubt if they received the wrong food or feeding time was delayed by too long, they would gladly express their temper. If only Sharon could hear the colorful insults from their mouths, it would surely cause her to hate cats even more.

"I never knew that story."

"Yeah, every time Sharon complains about being lonely someone always suggests getting a cat. That comment alone sends Sharon on a rant about why cats aren't allowed in her home."

"So is it that cats aren't allowed in her home, or she just doesn't like cats in general?" I quizzed.

"I think she just doesn't want them in her house. We have a stray cat that wanders around here and she feeds it. Plus, she goes to Mrs. Hastings' home all the time and Rusty is always there."

That was very true. Sharon was a regular at the gossip ring get-togethers because she always wanted to be the center of attention. Always had to be there to make sure their facts were in line, especially if they were going to be talking about her. Might as well steer the narrative if one had the chance.

"Thanks Ethan, that really helped!"

"No problem! By chance—"

I didn't wait to hear what Ethan was going to say as I headed toward the door. Sharon was officially off my list, and I needed to move on to the next person.

Chapter Thirteen

L ucy Walker rarely showed up to the gossip ring
get togethers unless she was bored. According to
her, attending the events made her feel old and she
was anything but old. Lucy lived a very active life and
because of that she had a routine. Around this time in
the day, she would be at the gym getting in one of her
multiple daily workouts.

Which made my next stop the gym. It was a nice
day out and gave me a chance to enjoy my time
outdoors walking to the gym as I mulled over how to
approach Lucy. I didn't have Rusty with me, and he was
the key ingredient in sniffing out the murderer. I'd
lacked a plan when I went to the café, but I got lucky
and got information out of Ethan. If Sharon had been
there, she would have pressed further, trying to figure
out if someone was talking about her. So maybe it was
good that she hadn't been there.

I turned the last corner, putting me on the street the gym was on, and there was a familiar figure already there. His tall body leaned against the wall by the gym, and his hands were stuffed in the pockets of his hoodie.

"Afternoon, Zack. How is everything going?"

I didn't want to ask if he was feeling better because one never really felt better after a death in the family. His eyes didn't greet mine but instead he kept staring off into the distance.

"Fine, I'm just getting fresh air."

"Understandable. Do you have any plans for today?"

That seemed to have grabbed his attention because he pushed off from the wall to face me. His body, a whole head taller than mine, effectively hid everything behind him from my sight.

"Why are you asking so many questions?"

"I'm just checking in on you."

"No one asked you to. Why were you searching my mother's cabinets?"

A lump formed in my throat. I had been so sure I'd played that whole thing off perfectly. Getting caught by Mr. Higgins and saying I was looking for extra raspberry sauce for the cheesecake had made sense, and the former detective even believed it! But if Mrs. Higgins had caught on, then others probably had also, and it seemed like Zack was one of them.

"Just trying to find some more of the delicious

raspberry sauce," I explained as I took a few steps back. Zack never seemed scary before, but he was starting to now. I did not want to find out what was about to happen next.

"I really need to get going!" I shouted as I sprinted past him to the front steps of the gym. After walking a few feet into the gym, I peered back outside at Zack who still stood on the street. He hadn't turned to watch me run off.

He stood just a few moments longer before he started to cross the street and headed in the direction of the flower shop. I let out a sigh of relief I didn't know I was holding. He was probably just in a bad mood as he tried to process everything, which was understandable. He just needed time.

"What are you looking at?"

My body jerked a few paces forward, almost sending me smackdab into the glass door that I was peering out of. Somehow craning my head over my shoulder, I let out a groan as I saw who was before me.

Of course I would run into Bridget Tanner here. I totally forgot she had taken a part-time job at the gym. She moved forward, peering over my shoulder to locate what had caught my attention out on the street.

"Got eyes for Zack? Didn't take you for someone that would be interested in a long-distance relationship, but it makes sense."

Confusion spread on my face. How does one not

get pegged as the ideal person to have a long-distance relationship?

"Could you clarify?"

Bridget leaned back away from the window, her arms crossed in front of her as her eyes scanned me up and down.

"You like being alone. Having a long-distance relationship would allow you still to be alone."

"Shouldn't a relationship make you not feel alone?"

"Yeah, but you are weird, so it makes sense you know?"

The big snort that left my lips was intentional, no need to hide it. Why would anyone agree and go along with that crazy nonsense of a statement?

"I've got work to do," she continued. "Are you here for any other reason besides spying on Zack Hastings?"

"Shh!" I hissed, as I looked around the gym to see if anyone had overheard us. Instead I zeroed in on the figure of Lucy Walker off in a corner, doing yoga with a few others.

"Why keep it a secret? No one but you would be interested in someone like him."

My eyes never left Lucy as I continued to talk to Bridget.

"Like him? What do you mean?"

"Whatever, I don't feel like talking to you anymore."

"Nice talking to you, too," I muttered.

I heard Bridget walk away. No idea what she was talking about, and I didn't have time to dwell on it as the next person on my suspect list was in front of me. She seemed knee deep in a yoga class, so I couldn't just walk over there and bombard her with questions.

That would be a sure way to look crazy, and if she became suspicious of all my questions, I wouldn't be able to glean any information from her. So I did what a real detective would do—I blended into the surroundings and spied.

The only problem was, this was a gym, and I had no idea how to properly work out. So if I didn't get sussed out by asking too many questions, I would surely get found out by having no clue as to what I was doing.

There wasn't really any equipment by the yoga studio, but I needed to be somewhat close by to overhear her conversation. My eyes landed on the row of treadmills; it was close enough. I made my way over there. There would be no way I could screw up operating a treadmill.

I craned my head forward as I dialed the button up to a fast walk, turning my ear toward the yoga area. I could clearly hear the instructor, who seemed to be extremely enthusiastic.

As I continued to walk on the treadmill, I kept my eyes glued on Lucy Walker. I could see her mouth moving, but I wasn't sure if she was talking to someone or cursing the workout under her breath— which is what I would have been doing if I was in her position. But when I caught the faint sound of her laugh, I realized I was too far away, and I needed to get closer.

"Walking buddies?"

A voice chimed in next to me, causing me to stop my effort to turn the treadmill off. I didn't recognize the person who spoke. She must have been new in town.

"Ah, sorry, I was just getting off."

"After three minutes?"

I laughed nervously as I scratched the back of my neck from all the nervous jitters forming. The gym had been a very bad idea, and I was already looking suspicious and out of place here.

"Yeah, I realized I wanted to do something else."

"Oh, okay, maybe next time?"

I nodded my head in reply but hightailed it out of there before I blabbed that I was here spying and not doing any gym-related stuff. I didn't even have a membership to be working out here!

As I walked away quickly, I looked toward the front desk where Bridget was leaning over the counter typing away on her phone. As long as she stayed glued to her phone and didn't notice me attempting to use the machines, I might be able to lurk a bit longer.

That of course would mean no more talking to the gym members, as they seemed to be able to sniff out fakes.

All the machines that were closer to the yoga area were equipment that seemed too intense. Like where you could break your back if you used it incorrectly. If I ended up getting injured from this adventure, Rusty would surely never hear the end of it from me.

The safest-looking machine and the one with very few people nearby was a leg machine, if the seat and board attached to the machine were any indication. I slid into the seat and waited a few seconds to see if I could catch any more of Lucy Walker's conversation from this new location.

And indeed I could, as I heard a few of the yoga students talking and of course the instructor going on about the benefits of each of the positions.

I planted my feet against the board and pushed. Instant shockwaves traveled through my body and a whimper escaped my mouth. I balked as I looked down at the weights to see how much I was supposedly trying to press. Whoever had sat here before me must have been incredibly strong because the amount of weight indicated was insane.

"You know, you are supposed to adjust the weight before you start using it."

Lifting my arms a little, I sniffed. Was there a smell about me that caused people to gravitate to me? A smell that just screamed *total newbie* and let them know that there was an imposter in the gym among them?

"Are you okay?" The guy's hesitant voice said, breaking into my thoughts.

My body crashed into the back of the seat of the

machine, and I plopped my head back to look into two pools of blue. It was a pair of blue eyes I had never seen before. If I ever wanted to meet new people, maybe I should hang out at the gym more often. Especially if this person was a regular.

"Hi," I said quietly as I stared up at him.

"Hi. Do you want some help?"

My head nodded on its own, and he maneuvered to the side of the machine where the weights were located.

"Let's start off light and see how that feels, okay?"

Another quiet reply left my lips, but I wasn't even sure if he heard me because I wasn't even sure what I had said. He picked a lighter weight and motioned for me to press forward with my feet, and I did. Instead of huge shockwaves traveling through my body, now it was small ones as my legs started to quiver at my attempt to push the board forward. The man scratched his head. He looked at my quivering legs. A blush spread on my face as he examined me.

"Huh, I guess we should go lighter. No problem."

Again he adjusted the weight and motioned for me to try again. This time no shockwaves, but my legs still quivered a bit. But pushing the board forward was easier than the last two attempts.

"Great! You should do three sets of fifteen reps."

"Okay."

I stared at him, hoping he would walk away and I wouldn't have to do those reps. I wasn't trying to work out, but he was so nice and cute, I didn't want to look like a complete fool in front of him.

"You do know what reps are right?"

I tried to not look like a deer caught in headlights. He gave me a confused look and my legs started to move on their own as I did my best to hide my embarrassment. I pressed forward, struggling to complete the required fifteen reps in the first set.

"Great job!" he cheered. "Take a few seconds and start up again!" He still stood by the machine.

My lips turned into a frown as I was forced to start the second set. What in the world was I doing? I was supposed to be here watching a suspect, and I was ending up working out at the gym for the first time since forever.

"Really, Kat?" Bridget's voice chimed in just as I finished the last rep of the third set.

"Oh, you know her?"

"Yeah, but the real question is what exactly she's still doing here?"

"Just trying new activities, expanding my horizons."

Bridget's face let me know she didn't believe a single word I had said. A shuffling noise next to me took my attention away from Bridget to the guy who was helping me. He had taken his wallet out of his pocket and was in the process of pulling a business card out.

Pushing it forward into my hands, he beamed a smile at me as I read the words on the card. *Lewis Hall,*

Personal Fitness Instructor. Ah, no wonder he was able to tell that I had no idea what I was doing. He was trained to spot people like me.

"If you ever need help working out, just let me know!"

"Don't waste your time. Kat doesn't work out," Bridget said, adding in her own two cents to the conversation.

"Why are you here? Zack —" The rest of Bridget's words were scrambled as I rushed forward and slapped a hand over her mouth.

With a smile presented to Lewis, I promised him I would call if I was ever interested in learning more about the art of working out. He seemed to get the clue that this was a conversation he probably shouldn't be included in anymore, and he took his leave.

"Stop mentioning Zack! I only looked at him for thirty seconds!" I hissed at Bridget.

"Yeah, which was only like thirty seconds ago. What are you still doing here?"

I paused before replying to Bridget and looked toward the yoga area. Because instead of a group of people doing yoga, now there was just the instructor putting away some of the equipment that had been used during for the class. No Lucy Walker in sight. Panic started to bloom in my stomach, since the whole reason I was here in the gym was no longer here.

"I've got to go," I blurted out to Bridget.

"Still don't know why you were here in the first place."

With a quick wave flung over my shoulder, I sprinted to the front door. I briefly met Lewis' eyes on my way out, and I tossed him a smile, which he returned. He was nice but I was a girl on a mission who had just lost her target.

Pushing the gym doors open and running to the end of the sidewalk, I couldn't see Lucy Walker anywhere. She had a routine, but I didn't know exactly what it was so I had no idea where her next stop would be. I could wander around, trying to locate her, but that would be a waste of time. I had no idea where to start.

A shopkeeper's bell went off in the distance, which caught my attention, and I looked over to where the noise had come from. Zack was just leaving the flower shop and walking away in the opposite direction.

Well if I couldn't find Lucy Walker, I could spend my time talking to the next person on the list—Fiona West, who was the owner of the only flower shop in town.

Chapter Fourteen

The sweet scent of flowers greeted my nose as I entered the shop that Zack Hastings had just left. Mrs. West wasn't at the front counter, which gave me time to roam around and explore. It also allowed for me to gather my thoughts and figure out how to question her about Mrs. Hastings' last brunch. I needed to figure out if Fiona could be removed from my list or if I could circle her name because I had found our murderer.

The flower shop wasn't big, but since not much furniture was needed to display flowers, it was still roomy. In the center of the flower shop was the ready-to-go flowers, already arranged in bouquets. Ready to be snatched up and taken home to a loved one.

Flowers lined both the left and right sides of the shop. But what was truly unique was that in the far-left corner was an iron spiral staircase that took you up to a little walkway, which led to a second floor. The second floor of the flower shop was an open space and allowed people to look out over the front of the shop. Because of this, it was Mrs. West's workshop. She could be away from customers but still keep an eye on her shop.

Heading over to the staircase, my eyes were instantly drawn to the blue and purple flowers on display in the middle of the shop. I did not know the names of the flowers, but the abundance of flowers around made everything smell heavenly.

The soft patter of footsteps coming down the stairs drew my attention away from the flowers. I saw Mrs. West descend down the stairs in her capris, T-shirt, and flower apron.

"Afternoon, Mrs. West!" I called out. She hadn't noticed me, so she jumped back a little, spooked at the sudden noise no doubt. But a smile soon spread across her face.

"Afternoon, Kat, how are you?"

"Not bad, just thought I would swing by and hang out for a few."

"It is always a delight to see you. And you just missed Zack!"

"I saw. I hope everything is going okay for him."

A pained expression flicked onto her face but it soon disappeared. She and Zack had probably talked about something very personal and she didn't want to let on to what that was.

"Would you like a cup of tea?"

I nodded my head in reply as she continued to make her way to the back of the first floor behind the register. She ducked down behind the register, and I heard shuffling sounds. A few seconds later, her head popped back up.

"All right, let's go on up." Mrs. West made her way to stand in front of me and headed up the spiral iron staircase. I followed, amazed at the beautiful sight of the flowers with every step I took.

Working at the flower shop one summer while in school had been one of the best summer jobs I'd ever held. It was simple work and it was peaceful. Mrs. West's knowledge and easy-going nature caused each day just to breeze on by. Which was a great relief from the crazy things going on in the world sometimes. It was like the flower shop was an escape.

We moved along the narrow walkway to reach the second-floor workspace. There was a small white, iron table and two chairs off in one corner. A tray with a teapot and cups was already set out.

"I expected Zack to stay longer but he dipped out as I was making the tea."

Nodding along, I pulled out one of the chairs out and sat down as Mrs. West poured tea into our cups. Taking a whiff of the steaming liquid in the glass cup set in front me, I could instantly tell this was a homemade tea because a few loose herbs filtered through and floated in the cup. Taking a sip caused a warm feeling to course through my body, and I couldn't help but smile.

"Could I get some of this mix to take home?"

"I always thought about selling my tea along with the flowers. But I was never sure."

"You should! This is very good!" Cupping both hands around the teacup, I brought it again to my lips and took another sip. The aroma flooded my nose as the hot tea dripped down my throat and warmed up my body once more. I refused to leave the flower shop without taking some of this wonderful blend home.

"It's a calming mixture, I hoped it would help Zack, but he didn't stick around to try it."

"Is he still tense?"

"He seems to not totally be present, which is understandable with the loss of his mother. But enough of sad talk. What can I help you with today?"

Oh, that was right, I had come here to question Mrs. West on the murder of Mrs. Hastings. But how should I go about it without seeming too obvious?

"I actually wanted to talk about Mrs. Hastings, but I understand if you want to talk about something else," I started off. I was hesitant to bring the topic back to the Hastings family when she'd just attempted to change the topic.

"Such a terrible thing to happen to such a wonderful lady. Did you know she was just as obsessed with her garden as I?"

"She did always maintain her garden. After all, she

always won the best yard every month." That caused laughter to escape from Mrs. West.

"That darn contest. I swear if Paula doesn't win it next, we are never going to hear the end of it."

This was my time to press on to see if she might have any useful information about Mrs. Hastings's death.

"Personally, I don't think she has a very pretty lawn so I doubt she will win."

Mrs. West's laughter continued on with my statement.

"Very true! Both Rose and Paula have a horrible green thumb. But what Rose had that Paula was missing, was Alec Ford."

I perked up as she spoke, I knew Alec took part time jobs around town to help out his family, and one of those jobs was at Mrs. Hastings's home. But I had always assumed it was to help her out in general around the house, like fixing things, since Zack was not around. But the mastermind behind the lawn was Alec instead of Mrs. Hastings this whole time? Paula would be sure to scoop up the young man next to have him working on her lawn in order to secure her position as the best lawn on the block.

"Alec has a green thumb?"

Mrs. West brought her cup of tea to her lips as she sipped and nodded her head in answer to my question.

"Oh yes," she said. "I taught him a few things, but he is just a natural. He really connects with the Earth."

"Did Mrs. Hastings seem off at the brunch? I can't believe she passed so soon."

Mrs. West took another sip of her tea and waited before replying. Choosing her next words, no doubt. "I don't think so. Everything seemed normal except Rusty wasn't present. He always tried to sneak some treats from the table and Rose would always give in."

So Mrs. West had noticed that Rusty was not present. Because of her comment, I had an inkling that she liked his presence and she would not have wanted him locked away from the guests.

"Oh yes, I heard something about that. Are you a fan of cats?"

"Yes, but having cats and a flower shop is hard. A lot of plants out there aren't safe for cats. And cats don't listen well like dogs, so there is too much stress to have both cats and plants in my life."

I nodded silently. It made sense. As a flower shop owner, she would be expected to carry a lot of varieties of flowers, not just those that were safe for cats. That may have knocked her off my list but I still had a few people left, namely the green thumb Alec and the evasive Lucy Walker.

"Do you know if any of your friends don't like cats? I'm trying to find a home for Rusty now."

"Poor Rusty, I would take him in if I could. But I happen to know the librarian Mr. Tempest is looking for a pet for his kids."

"Thanks for the information! I'll make sure to stop

by and check with him." I couldn't conceal the slight look of disappointment on my face. I had hoped she would suggest someone on the block so it would help narrow down my suspects, but she had named someone who was totally in the clear.

At least she made a good suggestion. Mr. Tempest was an exceptional man—a little grumpy and always going on about books, but an acceptable man, nonetheless. With the passing of his only daughter several years ago, he and his wife were left to raise her two children.

"I've really enjoyed this tea, but I should be heading home. Got some cats to feed. Do you think I could grab some of that blend to go?"

Mrs. West scooted back her white iron chair to stand up. After stretching for a moment, she headed to a table a little farther back in her workspace. She grabbed an already packaged set of tea and a sheet of paper before she headed back toward my way.

"Like I said, you are in luck. I had hoped to give this to Zack since he has been interested in tea blends, so I already had this packaged."

Grabbing the offered bag of tea and sheet of paper from Mrs. West outreached hands, I leaned in and gave her a quick hug before heading toward the stairs. I still had two suspects on my list and I couldn't dawdle in one place too long!

Chapter Fifteen

"Any luck today?" Luna's soft voice echoed through the home as I opened the front door. The drive back home had been easy and fast.

"Knocked one more off the list and now we've got two more to go. But honestly I feel like I'm doing this all wrong."

"Why do you say that?"

"Things just aren't adding up and I'm not sure why. There is a reason I didn't become a detective in the first place. Maybe this just isn't my jam."

"Never know till you really try."

Giving Luna a sidelong glare, I hung my keys up on the hook by the door. I would never really know till I try? I scoffed as I repeated those words out loud. If I wasn't trying, then what was I doing the past several days? Had I just been wandering around and questioning people for fun?

"Are we getting food?" Rusty's voice butted into my thoughts. Of course, that was all I was good for. A human to open the canned food for the cats and solve murders...again, all for the cats.

"I checked around and I think I found you the perfect place to live, Rusty."

"Will I get an endless amount of food there?"

"I mean, that is something you will have to discuss with them. I can give you some food now, though."

Going to the pantry that contained their cans of food, I picked one up and popped it open. Luna and Rusty were already by my side, but I could hear the patter of Zaira's feet as she bolted from wherever she had been hiding, so she could also get in on the food. I dumped the food into their cat bowls, and set them on the ground. While they munched away, I'd be able to clean up from the morning since I'd left in a bit of a rush.

When the last dish in the sink was scrubbed, rinsed, and set on the drying rack, I caught a glimpse of a very nice white SUV pulling into the driveway and then the garage of the house across the street. Lucy Walker's house.

She may have evaded me all day, but now that she was home this would be the perfect chance to go see if she liked cats or not. With only two suspects left, this would solidify and lock in the final suspect in the murder of Rose Hastings. Once I'd done that, I could find the missing cat then return to my normal life and not bother having to spy on my neighbors.

Before I could even dry my hands from all the washing, my phone began to chime. It wasn't the tone of a voice call, but the one that indicated a video call was incoming. And there was only one person who video called me. Dread filled my body as I stared at the picture of my best friend's face on my screen. I cast my eyes over to the cats, who still sat licking every inch of their bowls. Zaira, Rusty and Luna...but no Lola.

The phone kept ringing and I just kept staring at it while it chimed away. Eventually the phone stopped ringing. The call had ended. But no sooner had I let out a sigh of relief then it rang once more and showed my friend's face again.

Swallowing down my nerves, I picked up the phone and swiped to answer the call.

"There you are! I was wondering if you were okay!" My friend's voice greeted me.

"Oh you know, I'm just peachy."

"How is everything going with the cats? But more importantly, the death?" she asked.

"Death, murder, same thing. The cats are great." Hopefully she didn't hear the stressed tone in my voice when I mentioned the cats. I crossed my fingers that Lola was great. Everything was going to suck if she was somehow hurt or something had happened to her and I had to explain this to my friend.

"Murder? You don't say! Tell me more."

"I mean, we think it's murder, but I'm not sure yet."

"We? Mrs. Higgins has got her paws in it, does she?"

I wasn't sure what to say to that. It would make the most sense to say Mrs. Higgins was looking into it instead of the truth. But I'd already lied about Lola, and I would be adding on to that lie. However, trying to explain why I was looking into the murder myself seemed like the worst option. Because eventually I would have to explain that I could communicate with cats. Which was something she would want to test out on her own cats to really see if I could communicate with cats. But one of the cats wasn't here, and she would surely notice then. There would be no hiding a missing cat.

"Of course Mrs. Higgins is looking into it, who else would be?" I said nervously.

"Makes sense! Be sure she doesn't drag you into those crazy adventures she's always going on about. Don't need you on someone's bad side and ending up dead."

This time I couldn't force out a laugh to ease the awkwardness. It wasn't Mrs. Higgins who pulled me into investigating a dead body. It was my best friend's very own cat who'd escaped and gotten me roped into this mess.

"I'll do my best."

"So how are the cats? Hopefully not too much trouble!"

"Not at all!" I croaked out in response. Taking care of the cats was easier, especially since Lola was not here. But just because one was not here still didn't make it a walk in the park.

"Can I see my babies?"

My heart froze a little at her words and I was unable to think of a way to manifest a missing cat into existence in the next few seconds. I looked up and could see Luna staring at me, waiting patiently to see how I would get out of this situation. There was no escape though—I would have to confess and just hope my friend didn't die of a heart attack.

And if she didn't, then I could only hope she didn't turn around and murder me for losing one of her fur babies.

"Uh, well you see..." The words stumbled out my mouth as I tried to find a way to say I was sorry that one of her cats was lost in the wild. "There's been a bit of a, uh..." Scratching my chin in a nervous manner, I could see her expression changing.

The stress and anxiety was manifesting and causing my throat to become increasingly itchy.

"Are you okay? Is something going on?"

Wetting my lips a little, I tried to move my mouth to provide a response, but nothing came out. I opened my mouth once more and tried to form words, but again nothing came out.

"Uh...Kat, what is going on?"

Swallowing down the lump in my throat and taking a second to calm my nerves, I moved my mouth. This was the moment, and there was nothing I could do to escape from this anymore.

Before I could even utter a word, a loud knocking boomed throughout the home and made the cats to squeak in shock from the sudden noise.

"Someone sounds impatient."

The person outside definitely sounded impatient as they continued to hammer on the door, trying to get my attention.

"I think I need to go."

Whoever was on the other side of the door might have just saved my life. At the very least, they had bought me some time until the next time I was forced to face my friend again.

I waved goodbye to my friend and ended the call. I rapidly walked to the door to see who was making such a scene. Peeking through the peephole, my eyes landed on the form of Lucy Walker, still in her gym clothes. I stepped back and took a moment before opening the door. Why was she here?

"Finally, Kat! You really need to answer your door faster."

"Sorry, I wasn't expecting anyone to stop by."

"Well, are you going to invite me in?"

I stared at Lucy, still confused as to why she was at

my front door. I moved aside and motioned to her to let her know she could walk in. Wasting no time at all, she strolled in and went straight to my dining room table, where she took a seat.

"The husband and I are taking a trip to take in a week or two, can you house sit for me?"

"That was the urgent matter?"

"Of course, why else would I be here?" Again, I couldn't help but stare at the lady sitting at my dining room table, legs and arms crossed as she leaned back in the chair like she was at home here.

A soft meow not only brought my attention but also Lucy's attention to the floor. It seemed I did not need to think of a plan to sniff out whether Lucy liked cats or not, because she had literally arrived at my front door.

Lucy leaned down and started to pet Luna, who started meowing even louder at the attention she was getting. But as Lucy continued to pet away, she didn't sneeze once.

"I heard you have three cats now. Didn't think of you as a cat person."

"I'm not really a cat person."

"Well, why the cats then?"

"My friend asked me to watch them for a bit."

"Right. So about the house?"

"Sure. Just let me know when."

Without a reply, Lucy got up from her seat at the

dining room table and headed to the door. With a wave in my direction, she spoke as she passed over the threshold of the front door.

"Will do. Thanks again, Kat."

Chapter Sixteen

It was a sunny day, and the perfect day to discover who had killed Mrs. Hastings. The only problem I was having was that hiding in a bush was causing me to get itchy.

I wasn't friends with Alec, and we didn't talk often. He spent most of his time either with his family or working, but I knew of him and had run into him from time to time. Despite being close in age, we lived two very different lives.

Alec had his long curly black hair pulled back into a manbun and was currently crouched in the back garden of Mrs. Hastings' home, tending to the plants while I peered at him from the bushes located along the side of the home. He wore a simple white shirt, probably not the smartest idea when doing garden work, but it seemed to have stayed clean so far. Along with his white shirt, he wore a pair of blue denim jeans. A very simple outfit that didn't scream *murderer.* But murderers always wanted to hide in plain sight, after all.

My body tensed, and my eyes widened as I heard movement behind me. It wasn't a human because they would have made a lot more noise. This was quieter. I was so lost in my thoughts that I almost didn't hear it. The grass rustled behind me and the noise was getting louder with every second as it drew near. My eyes darted around trying to locate the source of the noise. As soon as I located the moving object, I wished I wasn't stuck in the bush and instead was safe at home. Or that I had just stayed oblivious to the approaching animal and maybe it wouldn't have noticed me. But when my gaze met his two beady dark eyes, he realized I knew he was here. No doubt the fear rolling off my body in waves helped him locate me, despite people saying snakes don't smell fear.

This one certainly had to, because he stared me down. Moving slower than before, he shifted a bit closer to my side of the bush. I knew nothing about snakes, like whether or not this one could be poisonous, but I knew snakes in general were not on my list of favorite animals. They actually did not even come close to being on the top five hundred, and I could not even name five hundred different animals at the moment.

The snake shifted again, its tongue poking out, tasting the air, getting ready to dive in and snack on its newfound prey. But that wasn't something I would be waiting around for, and as soon as it shifted again and it slid by my foot, I was stumbling out the bush screaming at the top of my lungs, which was the exact opposite kind of scene I wanted to cause when spying on a potential murderer.

But sometimes one must weigh the costs: get caught spying on a potential murderer or get stuck in a bush with a snake - and I had picked the safest option.

"Kat! Are you okay?" Alec screamed from across the garden as he made his way toward me. I pushed forward and clawed the rest of the way out of the bushes and onto the grass. But I did not lie down and breathe victory because I was still too close to the snake for comfort. Jumping to my feet, I bolted in the direction of the back door of Mrs. Hastings' home. It surely would not follow me into a house, so that was the safest place to go.

Alec caught up to me pretty easily. The fact that I'd avoided the gym for so long most likely played a part. Fear fueled my legs and allowed me to skip several steps as I jumped up to the back door. I jiggled the handle to open the door, but it did not budge. Crying out, I turned to Alec who had come to a stop at the bottom of the steps and was staring at me in confusion.

"I don't think that is the proper way to break into a home."

"I'm not trying to break in! I'm running from a snake!"

"Well, that would make a lot more sense. I wasn't understanding you with the jumbled scream and the random running."

"Right. Can we go inside?"

"We can't. I had to return my key when Mrs. Hastings passed away."

My heart was still beating like it was going to pop out of my chest. Willing myself to take a few deep breaths and calm my racing heart, I headed over to the one of the sitting areas in the garden but I made slow progress as I scanned the ground with each step, watching to see if the snake was nearby and waiting to attack again. When I ran off in fright, maybe it also ran off. Hopefully not in search of friends.

I made it to the center seating area, which did not have any bushes around it, and plopped down in one of the white chairs. Alec joined me and sat down too, his eyes still glued to me.

"So what are you doing here?" he asked.

It was a good question; one I wasn't sure how to answer. I couldn't explain hiding in the bushes and not making my presence known earlier without it being awkward. And if he was the murderer—and there was a very good chance he was, since he was the only one left on my list—I had to be careful with my words.

The other suspects hadn't been suspicious because they didn't do anything. But when one did something wrong and was covering up the fact, they would be more alert to people sniffing around.

"I was just in the neighborhood and thought I would stop by." I wanted to facepalm myself at my words because they made no sense. Of course I would be in the neighborhood, I lived across the street. I could also see Alec had picked up on the odd choice of wording by the way his eyebrow arched.

"All right all right. You caught me! I wanted some flowers for my house."

"Why Mrs. Hastings' flowers and not any from Fiona West's shop?"

So far, the words coming out of my mouth were not helping my situation. I really needed to think about my next statement carefully, because if not I would be in a rabbit hole I could not get out of.

"Just wanted something to remember her by, you know?"

"So you wanted flowers from her garden, that will eventually die?"

I leaned forward in my seat at his words. It made sense but it also seemed odd. Flowers were common gifts at funerals and for the families of the deceased. But the fact he'd mentioned death was odd, especially for him, since he was most likely involved with the death of his boss.

"It seemed fitting since she liked spending so much time in the garden."

Alec nodded his head slowly. His body was still relaxed despite seeming a bit cautious of my questioning.

I took a deep breath. It was now or never to see if Alec was the one to murder Mrs. Hastings. I had to find out the truth in order to close this out and find Lola.

"Alec, can I ask you a personal question?"

He shrugged his shoulders and said, "I guess," in response. He did not seem bothered by me trying to gather personal information from him. It was a good sign that he felt comfortable with me. Or it was a bad sign—maybe he was feeling very confident that he would not be caught.

"How was Mrs. Hastings as a boss?"

"Isn't it too late to be asking about how she was as a boss? It's not like she is going to be hiring anyone again."

"I mean, I knew her as one of the ladies of the gossip ring. So I knew a bit about her, but I always felt like there was so much more to her than people let on."

A smile formed on Alec's face at my words, like he understood exactly what I meant.

"You were always very observant of things Kat, despite you not showing interest in stuff around you."

My body tensed at his words. If anything, it sounded like words right out of a TV show where the detective corners the suspect and then the suspect turns blood crazy and attacks the detective. But those were TV shows and this was real life, so hopefully, that was not how this would turn out. Because if that was the case, I should have stayed in the bushes with the snake.

"Mrs. Hastings was definitely different. A lot of people on this street are odd and hide things about themselves. For Mrs. Hastings, it was the fact that she was rich."

My mouth dropped open at his words. I knew Mrs. Hastings had money because she was a widow and didn't work, but I had just assumed her husband had left her enough money or she got a huge payout from his life insurance, which allowed her to live comfortably.

"Rich? Like how rich are we talking?"

"Old money rich."

If my mouth could drop any more it surely would have. Mrs. Hastings did not scream old money rich. How could this be? In shows and movies, you could always identify people who came from money. Like money was ingrained in their being, and no matter what they did, money would stay in the family. But that wasn't the air Mrs. Hastings had about her.

"She never had a need to dip into the funds she inherited because she made her own money. But she told me once she had billions saved away that came from her family."

"Billions?"

Before now, I did not know why someone would want to kill little old Rose Hastings. But if she had billions in savings, it made sense. It was a pretty nice motive for murder. And Alec was looking like the culprit after all. He didn't come from money and while that alone would not make him a suspect, it was interesting that he knew of the money when pretty much no else had mentioned this little piece of information about our neighbor.

"Yeah, supposedly—" Alec was cut off by the back door flying open which brought both of our attention to the house. The once-locked door was now wide open and Zack Hastings was standing in the doorway staring at us.

"Alec, is this what you do all day when you are being paid?"

I winced a little at the shout from Zack. I could see from the corner of my sight that Alec had rolled his eyes in response. But he wasted no time in getting up from his seat to head back to the spot he was working when I first spied on him from the bushes.

"Talk another time, Kat? The new boss is a lot stricter."

Nodding my head to Alec, I proceeded to get up from my seat as well. Instead of heading toward the back of the garden like Alec, I headed to the side of the house. Very careful to keep my eyes peeled and ears on high alert for any movement to indicate the snake was still lurking around as I headed home.

Chapter Seventeen

Somehow, I had found myself once again at the table of Mrs. Higgins, drinking a cup of tea. I had headed home after leaving the Hastings's house but found I could not sit still.

My thoughts were unable to settle because I was so close to solving the murder. I had my suspect, Alec Ford. The motive was money most likely, but it wasn't concrete as I still had a hard time believing Mrs. Hastings not only had millions, but billions stored away somewhere.

The only thing left to do was to figure out how he did it, and get the cops involved. Two simple steps, that sounded really easy in my head but if this case had shown me anything, it was that things were more difficult that I thought.

Alec did not belong to the social circle of the block I lived on. He only joined the occasional event because he had only been employed by Mrs. Hastings and had yet to be hired by anyone else on the block. I highly doubted he was seeking other employment if he was able to get his hands on any of that money stashed away.

Most likely he would keep his routine the same to avoid suspicion till the death became old news and then he would be able to safely slip away. So I needed to catch him before he decided it was time to hightail it out of here.

And that was how I ended up with another cup of tea in my hands, sitting across from Mrs. Higgins.

"So Kat, tell me what you've found out so far."

"I think it's Alec."

Mrs. Higgins's eyebrow arched a little as she stared at me from across the table, no doubt mulling over the words I just blurted out and trying to think through why Alec was my prime suspect.

"And why him?" she asked.

"Well, supposedly Mrs. Hastings was filthy rich, like she had billions stored away somewhere. No one has even mentioned that before, but Alec knew about it."

"That would be a good motivation for killing Rose, if he knew about the money."

When I spoke of the billions, she did not seem surprised. It was just like any old news to her, as if she already knew this information too.

"You already knew she had money, didn't you Mrs. Higgins?"

She pushed a few of her curly gray hairs back behind her ear as she set her teacup on the table and looked at me.

"Of course. I told you from the beginning that she had to have been murdered."

"How did you know she had money?"

"I have been solving cases in this town for ages. How do you think I met my husband?" She spoke before following up with a laugh.

"When he retired, he made me promise to stop investigating too. But crimes don't stop. I just knew Rose didn't drop dead randomly, and I needed someone to solve the case for me."

"Why not go to the cops with your suspicion?"

"Because it's me. The cops and I have a history. They don't like being told how to do their jobs."

I looked at Mrs. Higgins in a new light. I always knew she loved being involved in the gossip around town and she kept tabs on a lot of people, but I had no idea that she'd once solved cases on her own when she was younger.

"So do you think I am right about Alec?"

"Do you think you are right?" she questioned back.

I nodded my head in reply. He was the only one that stood out from the list of suspects and he had motive. Who wouldn't be swayed at the mention of billions? I certainly would be.

"If you think you're right, you must lay a trap to catch him."

"A trap? Like what?"

"One must confess to a crime. You can't just proclaim he did it. If you do that, you lose all your cards, and that will make you lose the case."

"What should I do then, to lay a trap?"

"Well Kat, what does everyone on this block like to do?"

"But Alec doesn't live on this block."

"True, but he would surely attend if there was a gathering. He is a common face to most of us, despite you not interacting with him much."

"So, we need to get everyone on the block together?"

Mrs. Higgins brought the cup of tea to her lips once more. No doubt it had chilled from our long-winded discussion about the death of Rose Hastings. But still she took a sip from it, not bothered by the lack of warmth.

"How should we get everyone together?"

"First, where did Rose die?"

"At a brunch at her home."

A smile spread across her face and one started to form on my own as I caught on to her thought process.

"If Rose was murdered at brunch, don't you think it would be poetic justice to capture said murderer at another brunch?"

Chapter Eighteen

More people than just those who lived on the block attended the gathering, but I suppose it couldn't be avoided because once you tell one person about a party, that person tells another and so on. There was an endless train of invites, despite the fact that I didn't want to summon the entire town. Luckily the whole town did not attend, but a good amount of people did.

Everyone from my suspect list was at the gathering —even the man of the hour, Alec Ford. Today would be the day Rose Hastings' murder was solved, then Rusty would tell me how to find Lola. Once Lola was found, I could rest easily and go back to my boring life, minus still having talking cats.

I caught the annoyed expression on Mr. Higgins' face as he was forced to man the grill and feed everyone who'd gathered in his backyard. I had offered my home as the meeting place, but with all the wisdom Mrs. Higgins had, it would be odd for me to hold a party especially since I didn't socialize much.

It would have been too suspicious, so I was forced to leave the party details to Mrs. Higgins while I worked on spreading the word about the get together. Too bad this was a onetime gig and Mrs. Higgins was retired per se, because we made a great duo.

"Kat, over here!"

The voice had come from behind me. Turning to look, my eyes landed on Mrs. Higgins but next to her was Alec. A knowing smile was on her face. Her gray hair was pulled back today, instead of being free to flow in the breeze. She beckoned me over and I complied by making my way to her. She put her hand briefly on my arm and then turned to Alec with a smile.

"Kat will keep you company for a bit while I go deal with my grumpy husband."

With those parting words she took off in the direction of Mr. Higgins, who was letting out some choice words at his frustration.

"I heard this was your idea," Alec said to me.

"It was supposed to be a secret, but it's Mrs. Higgins party so I shouldn't be surprised."

"We never finished our conversation yesterday. You left empty handed, too."

"Right. The billions Mrs. Hastings has hidden away. Tell me more about that."

Alec turned to the table behind him and set his glass down. Picking up some of the finger food, he popped a few pieces in his mouth before answering.

"I honestly don't know much. But she pays me very well. Like way too well for some garden work, so I asked her about it and she told me not to worry about where the money came from. But then I was like, 'Ma'am no offense, but I don't want to get involved with any shady stuff,' and I was going to quit. But she explained that her family was the old kind of rich and all of it seemed legit, so I stayed working for her."

Okay, that was not what I was expecting to hear. Alec had known for a while that she had money. So why wait till now to kill her? But what was really alarming was that he didn't want to get involved with anything shady.

Was it because he wanted to make sure the money was clean? That had to be the reason because nothing else would make sense. If he truly wanted to avoid shady stuff, he would have avoided committing murder.

Doubts flooded through my mind. Could I have picked the wrong suspect? But that couldn't be... because he was the only one with motive.

There was no point in delaying any longer. I needed to find out if he was allergic to cats and get him to confess in front of others. It was the perfect time to ask, because heading our way was Mr. Higgins and Zack. It looked like they were refilling the refreshment table, as their hands were full of plates of food and a pitcher of juice.

"Alec, do you like cats?"

"That's a random question. But I'm actually not a fan of pets."

"So you don't like cats then?"

Alec scratched his head a little before answering my question.

"I personally don't want pets but I don't mind if others have pets."

My face scrunched up in confusion a the roundabout way he answered. I needed him to point blank tell me that he didn't like cats and it was because he was allergic.

"Right, pets. But what about cats in general?"

"Cats are fine, I guess. Don't you have cats now?"

I wanted to groan in frustration at not getting a direct answer.

"Right, so Rusty—" I started but was cut off by Alec.

"What happened to Rusty? Haven't seen him since she passed."

"Do you like Rusty?"

"Yeah, I thought he was a pretty chill cat based on the times I had to cat sit him. A little bit too food motivated, I would say."

The wheels that were turning in my head screeched to a halt. Alec had watched Rusty before?

"You aren't allergic to cats?"

"No, why would you think that? I've had to watch

Rusty a few times now. Especially when Zack is in town."

My body shifted as I looked at Zack, who had just finished helping Mr. Higgins restocking the table.

"When Zack's in town?" I hesitantly asked, just as he looked at Alec and me indifferently.

"Yeah, Zack is the one allergic to cats."

Alec had finally given long-awaited answer. The answer to the question I had been stealthily trying to figure out for several days. Because the person who was allergic to cats, was the person who murdered Rose Hastings.

"I never understood why my mother got a cat when I'm allergic." Zack chimed in.

Well, that sealed the deal. I couldn't take my eyes off of Zack as he walked away with Mr. Higgins. This was not how I pictured today going, not even close.

A hand waved in front of my face, drawing my attention away from the retreating form of Zack Hastings back to Alec.

"Earth to Kat. You okay?"

I was the farthest thing from okay.

Chapter Nineteen

When life gives you lemons, make lemonade, they say. But instead it gave me lemons and squirted me in the eyes, as this crime just wasn't making sense. Zack had killed his own mother and was currently surrounded by a sea of people who had no idea.

It was one thing if it would have been Alec, because I had expected him to be the murderer so when I proved he was the culprit, I wouldn't have been too surprised. But I had been totally wrong and was now left gob smacked on how totally wrong I was.

Here, I thought Zack was being moody and mourning the loss of his mother, but instead he had delivered the final blow to his mother and was going about his life.

Alec still stood by my side, munching on some food with a glass in one hand, totally oblivious that he had provided the biggest clue, which had opened his coffin and nailed another's shut. Oblivious to the fact his old boss was killed by his new boss.

Life was weird—and let's not forget to include the talking cats.

Slouching forward, almost like I was going to crumple and crash into the table, I steadied my breathing and tried to clear my thoughts. So Alec wasn't the murderer, no problem. Zack was the murderer, again no problem...if I could get him to confess.

"Alec, I need your help."

"Sure, what do you need?"

I stood up straight and motioned for him to follow as I started walking. We couldn't take days to get Zack to confess because he was only in town for a bit longer and would no doubt try to leave as soon as possible.

We headed toward where Mr. Higgins and Zack sat at a table conversing. Apparently, Mr. Higgins was no longer required to man the grill. I stood a few feet behind the chairs they sat on, making sure I could see them from the corner of my eye.

"Alec, you mentioned she paid you handsomely. Did you ever ask why you received so much for garden work?"

"I did, actually. At first, I thought she felt bad for me, my family situation and all. But I think she considered me a son in a way."

From the corner of my eye, I could see Zack slightly

choke on his drink. His body seemed to tense at the comment of Alec being considered a son. I knew the relationship between Zack and Mrs. Hastings was strained, which had caused him to spend so much time away.

What had happened between Zack and Mrs. Hastings to cause him to finally cave in and kill his mother? I needed to press Alec more, get him to share more intimate details in order to observe Zack.

"You must have had a very close relationship with Mrs. Hastings then."

"Yeah. She even told me she wrote me into her will."

Now that was new, juicy information. It seemed instead of wasting my time going through each suspect on my list I should have gone to Alec first, since it sounded like he knew everything. Mrs. Hastings had a will, which would make sense if she had billions tucked away. She had to make sure that money went somewhere and didn't fall into the wrong hands.

The conversation between Mr. Higgins and Zack seemed a bit strained, almost as if Zack couldn't keep focused on it. I could tell by the way he kept looking in our direction that he was no doubt too interested in the chat going on behind him.

Mr. Higgins tossed a look over his shoulder in my direction, finally acknowledging us, almost as if he knew the change in Zack was because of us and what we were discussing.

"Getting written into a will? You must be really lucky," I continued.

Alec scratched his head, apparently a little bit embarrassed by my statement. He was indeed lucky; it wasn't every day someone got written into the will of a person who had billions of dollars.

"I think it was more along the lines of hard work rather than luck. She said she admired my work ethic and motivation. Said it reminded her of her father, who, despite being rich still worked very hard."

Mrs. Hastings had treated Alec like a son because he reminded her so much of her father. If any comment should have gotten a reaction out of Zack, this would have been the one, and it surely was. It seemed the not-so-silent conversation behind him was triggering him. Hopefully he would make a comment soon, allowing things to unravel, which would then lead to his capture.

Looking at Alec, I observed him for a few seconds to see if he was picking up on the tension unfolding behind him. But it seemed he was just going along with the situation. Now Mr. Higgins was more invested in the things unfolding behind him, no doubt his old detective mind kicking in. He must have sensed something was amiss as he tried to rapidly catch up to what was unfolding.

Alec didn't need any more prompting to continue telling me about Mrs. Hastings. He gladly handed over more information about his relationship with the lady.

"We would always sit down for lunch and she would ask about everything. She shared a lot of stories as well."

"Glad one of us could have a good relationship with my mother," Zack said in reply.

This was it.

Zack had finally joined in on the conversation, no longer able to just silently listen. Now a big hurdle was passed, but we weren't yet to the finish line for a confession was still needed. With one toe dipped in the water, surely the whole foot would soon follow and Alec needed no prompting to respond to the jab that was offered.

"Ah, sorry man. I didn't mean to make this awkward."

"It was awkward the second you got hired."

Until now, Mr. Higgins was just trying to determine what was going on by listening. But I could tell he was fully invested in the conversation unfolding between Zack and Alec.

"You don't need to be so rude, you know? I didn't ask for her to be super kind to me. I was just there to do a job, after all."

"Oh, so you didn't act like the saddest human on the planet and force my mother to write you into her will?"

My eyes widened at Zack's words and Mr. Higgins was also shocked. It was no secret the relationship between Mrs. Hastings and her son Zack was strained, but for him to get so triggered by a few comments was an indication that there was way more to the strained relationship than both let on to.

"I did no such thing! She kept talking about setting up a rainy-day fund for me and I made a joke... Which led into her sharing about her family and that the rainy-day fund was a piece of her inheritance."

Zack got up from his chair next to Mr. Higgins, and I took a step back. His face was enraged and showcased his feelings to the world—no longer caring about hiding them.

Mr. Higgins stood from his chair but he spoke no words. I could see a few heads turn our way due to Alec's sudden shout and Zack's quickness at getting out of his seat. This wasn't good. But in a way, it also was.

I didn't want a fight to break out and definitely did not want another murder to happen. Granted, if Zack aimed to kill someone in front of a bunch of people, it would not do well for him. With anger comes loose lips, and this was unfolding perfectly and needed to happen. Hopefully when I explained all of this to Alec later, he wouldn't hate me too much. Baiting him to get in a fight with someone capable of murder was not something he would want to hear about.

"By writing you in, she was writing me out."

A slight gasp left my lips, and I tried to muffle it with my hands. It seemed money was the motivation after all. Zack was an only child and most likely the sole inheritor of his mother's money, so he had nothing to worry about. But with Alec entering the scene, his supposed secure and comfortable lifestyle was wiped out from underneath him.

"I didn't know about that! If I did, I would have advised against it. And now with her death what am I to do about it?"

"Yeah, that was supposed to be you dead and not her!"

The gasp I let out earlier was nothing compared to the one that escaped from my lips just then. Zack pushed forward and I instinctively went to reach for Alec to push him away from Zack's lunging grasp. But my effort was not needed—despite his years, Mr. Higgins still had his fast reflexes.

One moment, Zack was standing and trying to reach us and the next he was eating a face full of grass. Mr. Higgins used all his force to push Zack down and keep him down, which was surprisingly enough force to keep the younger man on the ground. I guess I wasn't the only one who skipped the gym.

"Zack, we are going to have to take a ride on down to the station and have a talk with some fellow buddies of mine." Mr. Higgins reached into his back pocket and patted around, as if looking for something.

Letting out a curse at not finding it there, he called for Mrs. Higgins, who strolled over with not even an ounce of surprise on her face at the scene unfolding out on her lawn.

"Honey, I told you to keep cuffs on you. Told you something exciting was going to happen today." From her pocket, Mrs. Higgins pulled out a set of silver handcuffs and handed them to Mr. Higgins, who wasted no time slapping them on Zack's wrists.

"Damn, woman. I thought I told you to stop meddling in things. Trying to drag me out of retirement, are you?"

Mrs. Higgins shot me a smile but I was still reeling from Zack's confession and all the excitement.

"I didn't do anything this time."

Mr. Higgins ignored his wife and led Zack away. Zack was surprisingly quiet for someone who couldn't keep his mouth shut a few seconds ago.

A light tap on my arm took my eyes away from the retreating figures of Mr. Higgins and Zack to Mrs. Higgins.

"Good job. We've still got to work on your detective skills for next time, though."

Next time?

Chapter Twenty

With the most eventful part of the party over, everyone resumed whatever they were doing before. I was sure that Zack and his mother would be the talk of the town for a few days. Along with his little outburst and strong dislike for Alec, gossip about Zack would definitely be going for a bit.

Now the murder was solved. Not officially declared solved, as that was the police's responsibility. I had finally finished solving Rusty's one demand and now could really focus on the important thing—finding Lola.

"Are you sure this is the right way?" I whispered harshly to the cats in front me. I could barely see them in the dark, despite one of them being orange.

"Not too much farther! We will be there shortly!" Rusty called out as he continued to pad forward through the woods that sat at the edge of my backyard.

"If I would have known she was basically in my backyard this whole time, I would have just started searching."

"Yeah, but that wouldn't have helped me."

I crossed my arms and let out a grumble of annoyance, Lola had been very close to home this whole time! That was calming but also very annoying.

A sharp yelp pierced the air as Luna tumbled forward after stepping into a deep puddle of mud.

"Tell me again, why am I out here?" She yelled as she tried to shake the mud from her long coat.

"You invited yourself."

Which was true, she had invited herself. Rusty had made some comments about the wonderful food in the wild and beautiful scenery, and Luna had gotten interested. I let loose a laugh as I realized she probably didn't know the world did not just give her everything on a plate when she wanted it. No, it required work and sometimes that work was dirty.

"Right, we should all stop complaining and focus on the task at hand. Finding Lola."

"We should be almost there!"

I sighed with relief, knowing we were finally bringing Lola home. Looking about, I took in the forest that sat at the end of my backyard and how I had not ever taken the time to explore it. Trees surrounded us everywhere but what was really interesting was the random items of junk dispersed throughout the forest. Almost like a few people lived back here. Hopefully it was just some neighborhood kids goofing off in the forest and not an actual village forming.

"Right there!" Rusty's voice broke through my thoughts and caused me to look toward our destination.

At which there was nothing but trees and Lola. I drew in my breath, held it for a second before voicing my doubt that Lola would be found out here chilling. But then again cats were new things to me, and maybe that was just what they did in the woods.

"She's here? I don't see her anywhere."

"Of course not, because she is underground."

Underground?

How would Rusty know the exact spot of where she was, and that she was underground when he spent most of his time in my home? Things weren't adding up.

"Rusty, how did you know where to find Lola?" I questioned.

"I told her about this place."

If there was a way to beat up a cat safely, I would do it. This crazy orange cat had known exactly where to find Lola from the beginning because he was the one who had told her about this spot! Instead of just telling me from the start where to locate Lola, he sent me on a wild hunt trying to find a murderer, which was ten times more dangerous than finding a cat.

"Rusty, we are going to have some words when we get back home with Lola."

He could see the annoyed expression on my face but he just provided a little smile in return, like there was still more to the secret that I didn't know. Rolling my eyes in response, I continued forward.

I crouched down to peer into the dark hole that descended downward into the ground. I couldn't see any type of movement. Unsure of how far the hole went back and if Lola was really down there, I refrained from sticking my arm down into the darkness. Instead, I called out to see if she would respond and when I did, I could hear rustling.

But the rustling wasn't from inside the cave, it was coming from behind us. I turned to face the direction of the noise and called out again to the cat. I didn't have to wait long before that crazy cat stepped into the clearing.

Picking her up immediately, I turned her one way and then the other, inspecting her for injuries. I tucked her in the nook of my arm and ruffled my hand through her fur to see if there was damage I wouldn't be able to see but instead hopefully feel.

"What are you doing?" Lola hissed at the unwanted attention I was giving her.

Ignoring her comment, I continued to inspect her, not satisfied with the searching I'd already done.

"Ouch!" Dropping Lola down to the ground, I brought my arm up to my face to inspect the damages.

Lola had swiped at me, and had gotten a few pokes in, which broke the skin but not enough to draw blood.

"I was just making sure you weren't injured and you injure me instead?"

"Why are you even out here?"

This was the most ungrateful cat ever. I had just finished solving a days-long murder case in order to bring her home, and she was wondering why I was out here looking for her at all?

"Well, your mother would kill me, so I need to take you home."

"I like being outdoors."

"You can be an outdoor cat when you go back to Mom."

I could imagine the gears in Lola's head turning, going over my words to decide if it sounded like a good deal—which apparently it wasn't, because she then countered with her own offer.

"How about I be an outdoor cat and stop by every now and then? To ease your human mind."

Crouching down, I stared at Lola. This time it was the gears in my head spinning as I went over her offer, which was actually a better deal than what I had proposed.

One less cat in the house and not getting in trouble with my best friend sounded like a pretty good deal to me. My only concern was making sure she stayed in one piece, and came back to the house every so often so my best friend wouldn't get suspicious.

"So...You will come back to the house every few days?"

"I swear."

"You will stay in one piece at all times? I can't explain an injured cat to your mom."

"I will do my best."

I paused for a moment to really think it over. It was crazy to allow a cat to do this. But it was also crazy to hear cats talking and for me to have solved a murder. So what harm could it be to jump further down the rabbit hole?

"You got yourself a deal!"

"Folks, it's safe to come out!" Lola howled.

From the bushes and the cave came additional cats. It was a bit hard to count them all, but there were definitely more than ten.

I looked at them and how they looked at Lola and followed her command. I figured it was better not to ask questions. The less I knew, the better I could act oblivious when something happened—which something was for sure going to happen if Lola was involved.

Chapter Twenty-One

Rolling to my side, I stared at my phone and waited for my friend to call. I mulled over the past few days. The house was quieter since Lola spent most of her time outside now. But she did return as promised in order to ease her human's mind and not cause additional stress in my life.

Life was nice.

"Why are you still in bed?" Luna's voice drifted from the edge of the bed. I hadn't noticed that she had walked into my bedroom.

Before I could even reply, the familiar buzz of my phone went off, indicating I was receiving a video call. Swiping on the phone screen to answer, I brought it up to my face and smiled.

"So, the murder is solved and it was the son? No way! That sounds more like a movie than real life."

Nodding my head, I went over the details of the past few days—minus the missing cat part—to her, even though I had already explained everything via text. Sometimes you just had to hear things twice in order to believe them.

"Did they say how she died?"

"Supposedly it was a plant that grows in the forest by Mrs. Hastings' home. Zack put it in her drink."

"Zack knows about plants?"

"Mrs. West was teaching him about plants. She thought he wanted a hobby in common with his mother, not that he was going to murder her."

"No way! Now that is absolutely crazy."

"Indeed, I would have never been able to figure that out."

"You'll get it next time! You just need practice."

I stared at my friend quizzically. There wasn't going to be a next time. This was a onetime deal in order to find her missing cat, not something I did for fun. I provided no reply to her comment, so she promptly changed the topic to something crazy that was going on in her life.

This had been a onetime thing...right?

Thank you for reading Tabby Trouble! You can find the next book Himalayan Heist here: https://www.irisleigh.com/home/cat-aunt-cozy-mystery/

About Iris Leigh

Iris Leigh stumbled upon the genre of cozy mystery by accident. Since Iris is easily scared she does her best to avoid horror books, tv shows, and films. But dying for some type of mystery without all the suspense to make her heart burst from terror was when someone asked if she had ever read a cozy mystery. Now she has fallen in love with the genre and started to write to bring her stories to life.

Make sure to sign up for Iris's newsletter to get updates about everything going on!

Website: www.irisleigh.com

Himalayan Heist

They say diamonds are a girl's best friend, but in my world, jewelry is a cat's best friend.

I like many things, but talking cats isn't one of them. *Especially talking cats.* Not even the Himalayan cat who thinks I'm for hire.

Some might call me delusional. Others might say I'm eccentric. Whatever the case, I'm not interested. Nothing will make me change my mind... until the home I'm housesitting is burglarized.

I can't just walk away. Despite my reluctance, I must work with the cats to find the burglar and retrieve the missing jewelry. But for the record, I'm still not working for the cats... *I swear.*

Order here! https://www.irisleigh.com/home/cat-aunt-cozy-mystery/

Himalayan Heist: Sneak Peek

The breeze was slightly chilly as it brushed against me. With only a thin jacket to block against the wind, it wasn't much, but luckily it wasn't freezing. My hands dug even deeper into the pockets of my pants as I continued my stroll down the street toward the café. People passed by but they were all too busy on their phones or talking to their companions to notice my approach.

"Hi."

"Hi."

I instantly responded, despite not being sure who was talking or if they were even addressing me. But if someone said hi in passing on the street, it didn't hurt to acknowledge it. It might make somebody's day.

"Are you Kat Jones?"

Now that was weird. My progress halted as I looked about, trying to identify who was talking to me. As I scanned the people around me, no one was looking my way, and no one had stopped walking. Everyone was continuing with their business. With one last look about to make sure I wasn't crazy, I walked forward again. But I soon paused as a thought popped into my head.

It couldn't be, but it technically could …

I could still talk to cats, but surely there wouldn't be a cat talking to me in public? I hoped that wasn't the case as I tried to swallow the lump in my throat that had formed from the crazy thought of a cat talking to me in public. A quick brushing sensation against my legs caused me to look down and into the blue eyes of a mostly white cat with brown fur around its face.

"Hi." It spoke again.

However, I would not respond to a cat, especially not out in public. That was what crazy people did, and I wasn't crazy. Nope, that wasn't me at all. Instead of continuing my walk down the street, I broke into a light jog as I tried to put distance between me and the cat. It wasn't full-on running because that would draw too much attention. I let out a slew of curses under my breath as I got a quick look behind me to see if the cat was following me. And unfortunately, it was.

"Go away!" I hissed, trying my best to keep my voice low but also loud enough the cat could hear me. I wasn't trying to draw the attention of the passing two-legged folks—I just wanted the four-legged one gone.

"But I hired you!"

"It isn't possible to be hired by a cat!"

This cat was crazy, and it was doing its best to make me out to be nuts as well. Why would a cat think they could hire me? I had never laid eyes upon this cat before, and I would definitely remember if I'd offered my services to a cat, which I had not.

"I already paid for your help to look into a robbery."

My feet skidded to a halt as I whirled on the cat, who had no choice but to stop in its tracks or run into me. My eyes narrowed as I stared down at the cat at my feet, and I crossed my arms over my chest. I did my best to seem menacing, but most likely I was failing. Most people wouldn't classify me as a scary-looking person ... unless I was hungry. That was a very different story. Regardless, I had to set this cat straight; I was a human who wasn't for hire.

"Paid for my help with what? Fish?"

"No, jewels."

I scoffed at the cat's words, and a laugh soon erupted. Jewels as payment? Now I knew for a fact this cat was a different type of crazy.

"Right. Do you see any jewels on me?" I asked as I brought my wrists in front of the cat's face, showing that they were bare. Next, I touched my neck and ears to also indicate they were bare and void of jewelry. "No, right? You didn't hire me, so leave me alone."

This time I didn't wait for a reply from the weird cat and instead took off in a sprint once more to get to the café. Thankfully, pets weren't allowed in most businesses unless they were a service animal, and there was no way I would claim any type of association with this cat. I would finally be safe from talking cats and be able to enjoy my day. The distance between the café and me was covered rather quickly. A talking cat was certainly a motivator for the increased speed. Without sparing a single glance behind to see if the cat followed, I strolled up to the counter to order a drink.

"One iced coffee, please."

I grabbed my card from my pocket and handed it to the barista behind the counter, who in return swiped it and handed it back. They followed up by sliding my iced coffee across the counter into my waiting hands. It probably would have been better to have a hot drink because of the slight chill outside, but I could never turn down iced coffee.

I let out a satisfied groan as I took a sip of my drink; the caffeine sent small jitters through my body. Now it was time to find my date, Lewis. Where was he? My eyes scanned the café till they were drawn to a hand that waved as it shot up into the air. I waved my hand in reply and hurried over to join Lewis at a table by a window.

"I thought you might have bailed." He motioned to the empty seat and sent a smile my way.

"Was I that late?"

"No."

"Sorry about that."

"No problem at all. Glad you could make it."

I had provided a quick response to his question but found that it was hard to engage in the conversation we were having for my attention was drawn to something outside. A four-legged feline with blue eyes that looked exactly like the cat from before.

"Are you okay?"

My body chilled, and my heart felt like it stopped beating as Lewis looked over his shoulder. He seemed interested in seeing what was dividing my attention.

"Is that your cat?"

"No, just a random cat. Don't pay it any attention."

"Okay." He turned back around to face me.

"How is your business going?"

The smile on Lewis' face grew as he spilled everything about the personal fitness venture he was starting to pursue. He had already landed quite a few clients and was getting his name known in the city as the go-to person if someone wanted to get in shape. I eased back in my chair and let loose a sigh of relief at successfully changing the topic so we didn't have to address the cat still watching from outside. Lewis excitedly kept going on about his business, it was getting easier to ignore the two blue eyes outside. Whenever I got tempted to see if the cat was still there, I would instead just look down at my drink.

"I'm really glad your business is going well!"

"Thanks! I didn't know it would be such a lucrative field."

I nodded my head along to his words while raising my iced coffee to have another sip. I didn't know how much personal fitness instructors made, but obviously it must have been a good amount based on his comment.

"Do you think—" He started but got cut off as there was a light thumping noise on the outside of the glass window.

The blue-eyed cat was now banging its paw against the window, making a scene and not seeming to care that they were being rude and interrupting my date.

"Are you sure you don't know that cat?"

"Absolutely sure."

The cat continued to bang against the window, even though I was giving it my full attention now.

"I hired you!"

The high-pitched voice of the cat barely filtered through the window. I glanced over to Lewis to see if he had heard the cat speak, but he gave no sign that he had. I wasn't sure what sign I was looking for to see if he understood the cat, but he wasn't freaking out.

If someone had heard a cat speaking, they certainly wouldn't be sitting calmly in their seat. Nope, the only crazy person here was me. I slid down in my chair as I slightly grimaced at the cat, who just kept thumping away. I wanted to die from embarrassment. With my elbow resting on the table, I raised my hand and shielded my eyes to block the cat from my view.

"So what were you saying?"

"I don't remember honestly, but I think that cat really likes you."

"That's funny, considering I don't know that cat."

"I don't think we can just ignore the cat," he said as his eyes stayed focused on the cat, who was still not letting up.

"Excuse me for one second. Sorry."

I pushed myself out of my slouched position in the chair with determination to get this settled once and for all. A few people in the café watched as I made my way outside to confront the feline. It was seriously being a mood killer, and it needed to go away.

"Come here!" I hissed out to the cat to grab its attention as soon as I got close enough.

"Finally! I thought my paw was going to fall off."

"Maybe you should have stopped a long time ago, then?" I bit back as my foot tapped against the ground.

"I wouldn't need to be doing this if you did the job I hired you for."

"Again, how many times do I need to say this? A cat can't hire me!"

"But I did."

My eyes rolled before casting my gaze down to look at the feline sitting at my feet. I needed this cat gone as soon as possible before people started asking questions ... if they weren't already asking questions. I let out a sigh. What had I done to deserve this?

"Look, talking to a cat in public is bad for my

image. I will help you solve whatever you supposedly hired me for but just please go away for now."

"Okay."

That was it? The cat turned on its paws and walked down the street, satisfied with my agreement to help solve whatever case they had hired me for. I let out an enormous sigh of relief at finally getting rid of the cat. I made my way back inside the café. Too bad for the feline that I had no intention of actually following through with helping them. I still knew nothing about this cat, so even if I wanted to find it again, I couldn't. It was for the best if we went our separate ways.

I made my way back over to my seat and slid into the chair, doing my best to make it seem like the last few minutes hadn't happened.

"Are you a cat whisperer?" he muttered softly, his eyes wide as he stared at me. Now that was a better name to be called than crazy, so it was a win in my book.

"You could say I am, in a way." I brought my iced coffee to my mouth and took a huge chug to finish it off.

I needed some type of distraction from everything that had just happened. I snorted at the thought that the cat really thought a feline could hire a human, which in turn caused me to release a choked cry as my drink traveled down the wrong pipe. It seemed cats might actually be the death of me one day.

Made in United States
North Haven, CT
15 April 2024

51346061R00095